The Gift
Finding Noel
The Sunflower
A Perfect Day
The Last Promise
The Christmas Box Miracle
The Carousel
The Looking Glass
The Locket
The Letter
Timepiece
The Christmas Box

For Children and Young Adults

The Dance
The Christmas Candle
The Spyglass
The Tower
The Light of Christmas
Michael Vey: The Prisoner of Cell 25
Michael Vey 2: Rise of the Elgen
Michael Vey 3: Battle of the Ampere
Michael Vey 4: Hunt for Jade Dragon
Michael Vey 5: Storm of Lightning
Michael Vey 6: Fall of Hades
Michael Vey 7: The Final Spark

✳ RICHARD PAUL EVANS ✳

FROM THE NOEL COLLECTION

GALLERY BOOKS

NEW YORK   LONDON   TORONTO   SYDNEY   NEW DELHI

An Imprint of Simon & Schuster, Inc.
1230 Avenue of the Americas
New York, NY 10020

First Gallery Books hardcover edition November 2019

GALLERY BOOKS and colophon are registered trademarks of Simon & Schuster, Inc.

For information about special discounts for bulk purchases,
please contact Simon & Schuster Special Sales at
1-866-506-1949 or business@simonandschuster.com.

The Simon & Schuster Speakers Bureau can bring authors to your live event.
For more information or to book an event, contact the Simon & Schuster Speakers
Bureau at 1-866-248-3049 or visit our website at www.simonspeakers.com.

Interior design by Erika Genova

Manufactured in the United States of America

1   3   5   7   9   10   8   6   4   2

Library of Congress Cataloging-in-Publication Data
Names: Evans, Richard Paul, author.
Title: Noel Street / Richard Paul Evans.
Description: First Gallery Books hardcover edition. | New York :
Gallery Books, 2019. | Series: The Noel collection ; book 3
Identifiers: LCCN 2019032745 (print) | LCCN 2019032746 (ebook) |
ISBN 9781982129583 (hardcover) | ISBN 9781982129590 (ebook)
Subjects: LCSH: Christmas stories.
Classification: LCC PS3555.V259 N653 2019 (print) |
LCC PS3555.V259 (ebook) | DDC 813/.54—dc23
LC record available at https://lccn.loc.gov/2019032745

ISBN 978-1-9821-2958-3
ISBN 978-1-9821-2959-0 (ebook)

To Diane. Thank you for the decade.

Noel Street

PROLOGUE

It's been more than forty years. In sharing this story, I've decided to include some of my diary entries from those days—not as much for your sake as for mine. I find that in retelling our stories, the recounting eventually begins to take on more credence than the actual truth of the event.

—Elle Sheen

Every story is a road. And on all roads there are potholes and bumps, detours and unexpected encounters. This stretch of my story took place back in 1975 in a small mountain town you've never heard of—Mistletoe, Utah. It was a harsher than usual winter, and everything, it seemed, was frozen—including my life as a single mother working as a waitress at the Noel Street Diner.

Then, on one of those cold days, something came along that changed everything for me. More correctly, some*one*. It was the day I found William Smith lying under a truck on Noel Street.

Nineteen seventy-five seems both like just yesterday and a millennium ago. It was a different world. In many ways, a different country. Gas was fifty-seven cents a gallon, and Foster Grant sunglasses set you back a five spot. Jimmy Hoffa disappeared, and the videocassette recorder appeared. Stylish women wore long print dresses and knits, and men wore polyester leisure suits in colors the fashion industry is still scratching their heads over.

New York City was on the verge of bankruptcy, while *Jaws*, *The Towering Inferno*, and *Funny Lady* reigned at the box office. The year's soundtrack was provided by the likes of the Eagles, Aerosmith, Alice Cooper, Elton John, and Queen, while a nation with just three television networks watched *The Six Million Dollar Man*, *Kojak*, *All in the Family*, *M*A*S*H*, and *The Carol Burnett Show*.

Just the year before, President Nixon had resigned in disgrace over the Watergate break-ins. America was a cauldron of social unrest, and demonstrations and riots were evening news staples. Some of those demonstrations were over the Vietnam War. Some were over racial or gender inequality. All concerned me. I was a single white mother with a black child whose father had been killed in Vietnam. Dylan, my son, was now nearly seven years old. He knows his father only from my stories and the few photographs I have of him.

Mistletoe, Utah, was an unlikely place to raise a black son. It was as homogeneous and white as a carton of milk. Dylan was not only the sole black person in the small town, he was the only one some of the locals—mostly farmers and ranchers—had ever met. I know that to you who live in big cities or in the South that seems hard to believe, but that's how many of these small western towns were.

Nineteen seventy-five was the year Saigon fell and that nightmare of a war ended. At least historically. Parts of it would never die to me, not even now as I write this. But it was that footnote in history that, perhaps, played the most significant part of that winter's story.

While global chess pieces were being moved around the board by the forces that be, my little world was following its own rickety path, which took a major detour that holiday season, starting with, of all things, a burned-out clutch.

Will it ever stop snowing? I wondered as I walked to the car. The snow had piled up to almost six inches in the driveway of our duplex. I hadn't shoveled; I didn't have the time. Besides, it was going to just snow more. I pushed the snow off my car with a broom. "Come on, Dylan. We've got to go."

"Coming, Mama."

Dylan, who was tall for his age, came out of the house wearing a red-and-green stocking cap that one of the waitresses at the diner had knitted for him last year and his new winter coat that, in spite of his size, was still way too large, the sleeves coming down past his knuckles. I had bought it that big out of necessity. He had grown out of his last coat in less than a year, and I didn't have the money to keep up.

"Is the door shut?"

"Yes, ma'am."

"Then hop in, we're late."

I laid the broom against the house and got in the car. As

I backed out of our driveway, the Fairlane backfired, which made Dylan jump.

"Someone just shot at us!" Dylan shouted. He was imaginative.

"No one shot at us," I said. "It's just the car."

"It exploded."

"I'll give you that."

The Fairlane had been left to me in my grandfather's will. It had been a blessing and a curse. It was more than a decade older than Dylan and things on it were starting to go, something I was financially not prepared to handle. I had just replaced the alternator two months earlier.

What now? I thought.

CHAPTER

one

To call that winter a junction in my life would be like
calling the Grand Canyon a ditch.
—Elle Sheen's Diary

I don't know much about cars, even my own—a '57 Ford Fairlane that collectors would die for today but that I couldn't give away back then. That morning as I started the car something felt different, which, from my experience—in both cars and relationships—was rarely good. And there was the smell of something burning, which was *never* good.

"Do you smell something?" I asked Dylan. He had sensory processing disorder—something we didn't know about back then—and was highly sensitive to smells.

"It wasn't me," Dylan said.

I grinned. "I'm talking about the car."

"It smells like burnt toast," he said.

I sighed. "Looks like you're going to be late to school today. We need to see Mr. Renato again."

"I don't like Mr. Renato," Dylan said.

"Why don't you like Mr. Renato?"

"He smells funny."

"That's not nice," I said, even though it was true. Mr. Renato smelled more like garlic than a roasted clove. "He just smells a little like garlic."

"What's gar-lick?"

"Garlic is something you put in Italian food like spaghetti sauce and pizza. I know you like those."

"Yeah."

"Mr. Renato is Italian, like pizza. And if you say anything about how he smells in front of him, I'm going to ground you from watching TV for a whole week."

I looked over to see if he was getting it. He was frowning. "Can I tell him he smells like a garlic?"

"No!"

Mr. Renato owned Renato's Expert Auto Repair, but since his was the only auto body shop in Mistletoe, everyone just called it Renato's—a name that outsiders often mistook for an Italian restaurant.

Renato was of direct Italian descent, immigrating to America when he was nineteen. Like everyone else in town, including me, you had to wonder how he ended up in Mistletoe. It was a woman, of course. He met her in the bustling metropolis of New York and followed her back to a town so small that the McDonald's had only one arch. Actually, that's not true. We didn't have a McDonald's.

That was a joke. I had a whole repertoire of "our town is so small" jokes, mostly shared with me by truck drivers passing through. I've heard them all. *This town is so small that all the city limits signs are on the same post. A night on the town takes six minutes. The New Year's baby was born in September.* (That last one was actually true. Not a lot of births in this town, as most people leave to get married. I'm a sad example of what happens if you don't.)

The truth was, Mistletoe was so small that even people in the state of Utah didn't know it existed. Renato's love interest eventually left—both him and Mistletoe—but Renato stayed put. Unfortunately, my car kept us in frequent contact.

Renato's shop was on the way to Howard Taft Elementary, Dylan's school. The repair shop had three bays and a front office that perpetually reeked with the pungent scent of new tires.

"It smells in here," Dylan said as we walked in. I wasn't sure if it was a reference to the tires or the shop's proprietor.

I gave him a stern glance. "Remember what I told you. I mean it."

"Yes, ma'am."

"What you're smelling are the new tires. I like it."

"You're weird."

"No one's going to argue that."

Just then a short, olive-skinned man walked out of a back office holding a clipboard. He had a pen tucked behind his ear, partially concealed by his salt-and-pepper hair. He wore a long-sleeved, oil-stained cotton work shirt with an embroidered patch with his name on it. His hands were clean, though permanently dyed by motor oil. He smiled when he saw me.

"*Ciao, bella.*" He walked over and kissed me on both cheeks. "You are too beautiful."

It was nice to hear, even from Renato, who was a living, breathing Italian caricature and pretty much said it to every woman he encountered.

I was pretty in a simple way. Or, at least, I used to be. I was raised in the small town of Cedar City, the only daughter of a military officer turned rancher, and looked as wholesome as my beginnings suggested. I looked like my mother, which, I suppose, was a good thing, as she had been chosen Miss Cedar City in her youth. I had flaxen hair, a small mouth, but full lips and large brown eyes. I was trim, with curves. I wasn't tall, but, at five foot five, I was still taller than my mother. My height was something I got from my father, who was six one.

My father used to say, "I prayed to God that my daughter would be pretty, but not too pretty. Too pretty messes up one's head." Then he'd wink and say, "But God doesn't always give us what we ask for." He also used to say, "Pretty is as pretty does." I'm still not totally sure what that means.

No matter the standard, I didn't feel very pretty in those days. In the mirror of my self-image I just saw a lonely, quietly desperate woman hidden behind a mask of exhaustion.

"Hi, Renato."

He smiled even more broadly, the furrows on his face growing still deeper. "*Mamma mia, sei troppo bella,*" he said, sighing dramatically. Pretty much everything he did was dramatic. "Every time I see you it reminds me that I was born twenty-five years too early."

"Maybe I like older men."

"*Perché mi stuzzichi.* How you tease an old man." He glanced down at Dylan. "How are you, *bambino?*"

"My name's not 'bambino,'" Dylan said.

Renato smiled. "*È vero.*" He looked back up at me. "What brings you to my shop, *bella?*"

"The usual," I said. "My car's acting up again."

"Your curse, my blessing," he said. "Your naughty car brings you back to me. What is the problem this time?"

"Our car exploded this morning," Dylan said.

"*La machina cattiva.*" Renato looked out the glass door toward my car. "The car exploded?"

"It backfired," I said. "But that's not the problem. I think it's the clutch. It doesn't feel right."

"What does it feel like?"

"It feels . . . kind of loose. And it smells bad."

"You said something smells bad," Dylan said. "You said not to say that." I closed him down with a glance. I turned back to Renato.

"It smells like something is burning."

Renato frowned. "That is not good. Do you ride the clutch?"

"I don't know what that means."

"Do you keep your foot on the clutch when you drive?"

"I don't think so."

He breathed out loudly. "Your clutch may be going out on you."

"That sounds expensive," I said anxiously. "Is that expensive?"

He nodded side to side, then raised his hand to explain. He always used his hands to speak. (How do you shut up an Italian? You tie up his hands.) "The clutch plate is only twenty-five dollars."

"Thank goodness," I said. "I can almost afford that."

"It is not the part that is the problem," Renato said, his face pressed with pain. "Replacing the part is the devil. That is what costs the money."

"How much?" I asked.

"Usually costs about five hundred."

My stomach fell. It might as well have been five thousand. "Five hundred?"

"I'm sorry, but do not panic yet. I will have my man check it out first. You have your keys?"

"Right here." I fished my keys from my purse, which was a little embarrassing since my key chain weighed about a pound and had two massive plastic key chains that Dylan had made for me at school that said "World's Best Mom."

Renato smiled at the bundle. "Good thing you have a big purse," he said.

"I wish it was to hold all the money I had."

"We should all have that problem," he said. "I'll have William check your car."

"Who's William?"

"He is my new guy."

"What happened to Nolan?"

7

"Nolan left."

"Left? He was here forever."

"Thirty-three years. I am not happy about it. He moved back to Montana to raise cattle on his brother's ranch. Fortunately, this man, William, showed up two days before he left. He used to be a mechanic in the army." He walked to the door to the garage and opened it. Somewhere in the garage a radio was playing Simon and Garfunkel's "Sound of Silence."

"William."

A man I guessed to be about my age looked up from beneath the hood of a car. It was rare to see a new face in town outside the diner. He was tall, thin, with dark brown hair and dark features. Ruggedly handsome, I guess. At least I thought that at first. It didn't last long. "Yes, sir," he shot back, like he was still in the military.

"I love it when he says that," Renato said to me. He turned back to his man. "I need you to check the clutch on a Fairlane."

"Yes, sir. Keys in the ignition?"

"I have them." He threw him my bundle. The man caught them.

The man, William, suddenly looked at me and Dylan with a strange expression. As the mother of a nonwhite child, I was used to this. "I'll need to take it around the block."

"Of course," I said, like I had any idea what he needed to do.

He opened a bay door and walked out to my car.

"He is going to take it for a drive so he can feel the clutch," Renato explained.

"Or smell it," I said.

Dylan looked at me and I shook my head.

"Can I have a gumball?" he asked.

"Let me see if I have a penny." I reached in my purse and took out my change purse. It was mostly filled with pennies. "There you go."

"Thank you." He ran to the gumball machine.

"He is such a polite boy," Renato said. "He has a good upbringing."

"Thank you."

About five minutes later the new guy pulled my car into one of the bays and climbed out.

"What do you think?" Renato asked.

"It's definitely slipping," he said. "I can smell it."

I frowned. "That's what I said."

I looked at Renato hoping for some good news but he only frowned. "I am sorry, *bella*. It is going to need a new clutch."

My heart fell. It seems I was always paying for something. I had just finished paying off the alternator. Now this. And Christmas was coming. "Can you fix it?"

"Of course. I'll work with you on the price. I will give you the family discount. Can you make payments?"

"How much would you need?"

"I can do fifty dollars a month. I will do the tune-up for free, no charge."

"Okay." I didn't have a choice. Dylan and I were barely

making it as it was. I'd have to pick up an extra shift each month just for the clutch and pray something else didn't give out. Or that I didn't.

"Thank you," I said softly.

"*Prego, signorina.*"

"How long will it take to fix?"

"Maybe four to six hours. William is a fast worker. Can you leave it with me?"

"I kind of need a car. You don't have a loaner, do you?"

"Not today. I will have one tomorrow morning after Mr. Anderson picks up his car."

"Will my car last another day?"

"William, how much longer can she drive her car?"

"The clutch probably has a week or two left on it."

"Will I damage the clutch more?" I asked.

Renato shook his head. "The damage is done. But if it goes out completely you could damage your engine."

Just then William shouted, "Hey! Get off that!"

I spun around. He was shouting at Dylan, who was standing on top of an oily machine next to a stack of tires. "That's not a toy."

Dylan was paralyzed with fear. He wasn't used to being yelled at. I walked over to him. "Sorry," I said to William. "He doesn't know better."

"Then you should keep an eye on him. This isn't a playground."

"I'm sorry," I said again. I turned to Dylan, who was still cowering. "Come on, Dylan. Let's go. Don't touch anything." *So much for Mr. Rugged Good Looks*, I thought.

"He's scary," Dylan said as I took his hand.

"Yeah," I said under my breath. "Very." I walked Dylan back into the front office. Renato was already there behind his counter writing on a pad.

"So here is the work order. We are going to replace your clutch and give you a free tune-up."

"So this new guy of yours. Mr. Personality."

Renato looked at me. "Mr. Personality?"

"How's he working out?"

"William is a hard worker," Renato said. "He is doing a very good job."

"But not much of a personality," I said.

Renato's expression didn't change. "Do not be too quick to judge."

I wasn't sure how to handle Renato's uncharacteristic seriousness. And I was still reeling a little from his employee reprimanding my son and me, as well as the devastating financial news. "I'll see you tomorrow."

Renato nodded. "I am sorry for the bad news, *bella*. But I will give you the family discount."

"Thank you."

As I left the place, it was all I could do not to cry. *Why couldn't I catch a break?*

CHAPTER

two

These are days when I feel like Sisyphus of Greek legend,
forever pushing the stone up the hill. But I mustn't stop.
My son's future is at the top of that hill.
—Elle Sheen's Diary

As I pulled out of Renato's, the Fairlane seemed to drive even worse, though I'm not sure if it really was or if it was just that now I really knew something was wrong with the car and was looking for it.

Dylan was still quiet as I pulled into the school parking lot.

"You okay?" I asked.

He nodded unconvincingly.

"That was kind of scary to be yelled at," I said.

He nodded again. "I wasn't going to break anything."

"Maybe he was just afraid you were going to break yourself." I didn't believe it, but it didn't matter. I wasn't protecting the jerk, I was protecting my son. And he was probably just another bigot. I parked the car in the vacant bus lane in front of the school, then turned to Dylan and held out my hand. "Spit out your gum."

"But it still tastes."

"You know they don't allow gum in school."

He spit it out into my hand. I wrapped it in a tissue and put it in my purse. "Come on. School waits for no one."

Dylan was more than a half hour late for school so I had to sign him in. I held his hand as we walked into the front office.

"Good morning, Elle Bell," the school secretary, Cheryl, said brightly. Much too brightly for where my mind was.

"Morning, Cheryl," I said, purposely leaving off the *good*.

"Late start?"

"Car problems."

She shook her head. "Again?"

"Different ailment, same car."

"I have the same problem with my husband," she said. "Dylan, please take this note to Mrs. Duncan." She handed him a pink slip of paper. Dylan turned to go.

"Wait," I said. "What about my kiss?"

Dylan looked embarrassed, furtively glancing around to see if anyone might see him.

"Come on. No one's around."

He screwed up his mouth. "All right."

He quickly pecked my cheek. I pulled him into a big hug that he tried to escape from. I released him. As he backed away from me I said, "Don't forget your lunch." I handed him a brown paper sack. "I'm working late tonight. Fran will be picking you up from school. You got that?"

"Bye, Mom." He ran out of the office.

"He's a good boy," Cheryl said.

"Probably the one thing in my life that's not going wrong," I said.

"Well, if you had to choose something to not be broken, that's the thing."

I drove from the school to the diner. I could smell my burning clutch as I got out of the car. As usual I parked behind the restaurant and walked in through the back door.

"Sorry I'm late," I said, shutting the door behind me.

Loretta, the diner's owner, looked up at me. "Everything okay?"

"No. Another car problem."

She shook her head. "Is it serious?"

"Five hundred dollars serious."

She frowned. "I'm sorry."

"Me too. Just when I get one bill paid off, another pops up."

"Pray for big tips."

"I already am," I said. "If they don't pick up I'm going to be short on next month's rent."

"I'm sorry, baby," Loretta said. "Miracles happen."

"I could use a miracle right about now." I put on my apron. "But I won't be holding my breath."

CHAPTER

three

I always knew this day would come. So why was I
so unprepared? I suppose it's the nature of humanity to
avoid contemplating unpleasant inevitabilities. Which is
why so few buy their own grave plots.

—Elle Sheen's Diary

I t was a normal day, as far as my days went, made up of the usual mix of regulars and strangers—elderly locals who were lonely or bored, as well as the occasional trucker. Like my clientele, my schedule was equally predictable. When I worked the late shift I got home from work at ten—eleven on weekends. When I walked in that night, Fran, my sitter, was sitting at the kitchen table doing homework. Fran went to school at Weber State during the day to study music, evidenced by the violin case on the floor next to her. Fran was lovely, with an eclectic taste in music. I never knew what she'd be playing on her 8-track player when I got home—Chopin or Bob Dylan. Tonight there was neither as she was intent on her studies.

"How was he?"

"Amazing as usual. He made this for you."

She held up a blue-green marbled ball of Play-Doh, with toothpicks sticking out, four on the bottom, two on top.

I took it from her. "What is it?"

"It's a reindeer," she said, grinning. "Can't you tell?"

I grinned back. "I love it."

"He loves you." She put her homework in a bag and then said, "I should probably tell you, Dylan asked me something different tonight."

I looked up from the reindeer. "What?"

"He asked if Santa was a Negro."

It was the first time he'd used that word. "What did you say?"

"I said, Santa is a spirit. He's the color of giving. I don't know what that means, but he seemed good with that. I hope that's okay."

My eyes watered. "Thank you. You said the right thing."

"He's a sweet boy."

I gave Fran a hug. She picked up her case and walked to the door. "See you tomorrow."

"Good night."

I walked to Dylan's room and opened the door. As usual, he was asleep, the covers pushed down to his waist. Fran was right; he was a sweet boy. He was also a beautiful boy. He had light, mocha-colored skin and was lanky and handsome like his father, though with the more subtle facial features from my Swedish-Welsh heritage. He was exotic looking, as he had blue eyes, something that people would sometimes stare at in disbelief. One time a woman asked me if his eyes were "real." I didn't answer her. I still have no idea what she meant by that.

I lifted the covers up to his chin and kissed his forehead. "I love you, little man." I shut his door, then went to my room and undressed.

Where had he heard the word *Negro*? I wasn't surprised that he'd asked. As the only black person in an all-white farming town, it was only a matter of time. I just hoped I'd be a little better prepared.

The next morning I got Dylan up and while he ate breakfast I made his usual sack lunch—a peanut-butter-and-jam sandwich, chips, and the donut I brought home every night from the diner. I checked my watch and then said, "C'mon, sport. Time to go."

"Can I watch *Fat Albert*?"

"You know better than that. It's time for school. After school you can watch TV."

As we climbed into the car Dylan asked, "Will our car explode again?"

"I don't know. It might." I pulled out into the snow-covered street. "That reminds me. I'm not going to be in the same car tonight."

Dylan's face grew animated. "Are we getting a new car?"

"No. We're just borrowing a car until Renato fixes ours."

He frowned. A few moments later he asked, "Mom, what's a Negro?"

I looked over at him. "Where did you hear that word?"

"Marsha at school says I'm a Negro."

Take a deep breath. At least I knew where he'd learned it. "Well, that means you're super smart and very handsome."

Dylan looked confused. "She said I'm a Negro because my skin is brown."

"Well, that's part of it," I said. "Of course, everyone has different colors on their body. Some have different color hair, different color eyes, some have different color skin."

"She said I can't go to her house because I'm a Negro."

I bit down. "Well, there you go. People at Marsha's house must not be very smart or handsome, so they're intimidated by you."

"What's inti . . . date?"

"Intimidate. It means to be scared."

"Why are they scared?"

"Because they're not as smart or handsome. Did you even want to go to Marsha's house? It doesn't sound like a very fun place to be."

"She's having a birthday party."

I tried not to show my anger. I sighed heavily. "Some people are just . . ." I stopped short of calling her dumb. ". . . don't get out much," I finally said. I pulled up to the curb of the drop-off zone. "I love you, buddy."

"Love you too, Mom."

I watched him walk up to the front of the school and fall in with the other kids, all of them white. As I pulled away I started to cry.

I drove over to Renato's and sat in the parking lot until I regained my composure. I wiped my eyes and then walked into the garage's office, a spring-loaded bell above the door announcing my entrance. To my dismay, the new guy, William, was standing at the counter. I stiffened at the sight of him. I still hadn't forgiven him for scaring Dylan. Or me. After this morning I was especially sensitive.

"Good morning, Elle," he said with surprising gentleness. Even more surprising was that he knew my name.

"Is Renato here?"

"No. He won't be in until this afternoon. But he told me you would be bringing your car in this morning. He has a loaner for you. It's that green-and-white Plymouth Valiant out there." A smile crossed his face. "I know what you're thinking. It's too sexy to drive."

I almost smiled but didn't want to encourage him. "Thank you. How long will my car take?"

"I'll have it done by three," he said. "That includes the tune-up. That won't take much time."

"What time do you close?"

"Five."

I frowned. "I don't get off work until eight. Can I pick it up tomorrow?"

"No problem."

"And the Valiant?"

"There's no hurry on that. We don't need it."

"Thank you."

He handed me the keys to the loaner, which had somehow been connected to a golf ball with a bright yellow smiley face beneath the trademarked phrase "Have a Nice Day."

I smiled at the sight of it. Someone had a key chain almost as impractical as mine. "This is . . . unusual. Not as big as mine, but unusual."

"Keeps it from getting lost."

As I turned to go, he said, "I'm sorry I got mad at your son yesterday. The machine he was playing on could have hurt him. I'm just a little jumpy. I didn't mean to upset him. Or you. Please forgive me."

I looked at him. He was definitely sincere. There was also a vulnerability to him that I hadn't seen the last time.

"Thank you for watching out for my son. As well as the apology."

"You're welcome."

"So Renato will be back this afternoon?"

"He said he would. He'll call when it's done."

"Thank you."

"One more thing. The driver-side door on the Valiant sticks a little. You just need to give it a good tug. Oh, and the brakes are a little touchy. They're fine, just a little sensitive."

Like me, I thought. "Thanks for the warning."

I walked out to the Valiant, which had a two-tone paint job, an olive-green body with a white hardtop. As warned, the door stuck. I yanked it open and climbed in. Whoever had driven the car last was at least half a foot taller than me, as my feet didn't even reach the pedals. I adjusted the seat, put on my seat belt, then started the engine. It roared like an injured lion.

Some sexy, I thought.

As I drove to work, I prayed that the Fairlane's clutch wouldn't be as bad as they thought. I knew there was no hope for it, but I prayed anyway.

"How's it going, Jamie?" I said, walking into the diner. Jamie was the waitress I worked with most. She was five years older than me and off-and-on married so often that I sometimes forgot her marital status. She was born in Mistletoe and had worked at the diner since she was sixteen. She was now thirty.

"You know, different day, same problems. You got a new car? Those Valiants are crazy sexy."

I laughed. "No, I didn't get a new car. It's a loaner Renato gave me while he fixes mine."

"Oh, right. Loretta told me your car was on the fritz. You should have had Mark look at it. Maybe he could have fixed it." Mark was her second ex-husband, though she often acted like they were still married. Actually, that was true of her relationship with all her exes.

"It's the clutch. It's no easy fix."

She shook her head. "You can't catch a break, can you?"

"Not lately."

"Well, I'll pray for large tips. For both of us." As we walked out into the dining room, Jamie's eyes widened. "Oh, no."

"What?"

"Ketchup Lady is back."

I groaned. "I'm starting my shift with Ketchup Lady. Can this day get any worse?"

"Sorry, honey. I'd take her, but you know she's headed to your station."

"It's okay. I'll eat the frog."

"What frog?"

"You know the saying. Start the day eating a frog and nothing worse will happen to you all day."

"If only," she said. "I'd eat a frog omelet every day."

I watched as the Ketchup Lady, as usual, walked past the PLEASE WAIT TO BE SEATED sign and sat herself at the table she had claimed as her own. Actually, she sat at the table next to the one she usually sat at, though not without a brief attempt to reclaim her territory. For almost a minute she just stood looking at the people sitting at "her table" when one of the men—a burly trucker—looked over and asked her what she wanted. Without answering, she turned away and sat down at the next table.

No one knew the woman's name or where she lived. She had shown up at the diner the previous spring and had stopped by every week since. We called her Ketchup Lady because she put ketchup on everything, from pancakes to fried chicken and mashed potatoes. Her plate looked like a crime scene. The first time I took her order I gagged as I brought it out from the kitchen. None of the waitresses were fans, which had less to do with her culinary affinity than her personality, which, at times, was as nasty as her palate.

This morning she was wearing a red T-shirt that read:

I Like Ketchup
On My Ketchup

I walked up to her table. "Good morning," I lied. "What can I get for you today?" *Besides ketchup.*

She looked at me as if she'd never seen me before. "What *may* you get for me? Learn proper grammar, you'll go further in life. I'd like the ham-and-cheese omelet smothered in ketchup. Also a side of sausage—patties, not links—with ketchup. And your buttermilk biscuits with ketchup."

The biscuits were a new addition to her culinary repertoire. The idea of putting ketchup on a biscuit made me sick.

"We have a policy that we don't put things on our biscuits," I said. It was a policy I had made up on the spot. "But you're welcome to put anything in it you like."

She looked annoyed. "Then I'll need an extra bottle of ketchup. This one is nearly gone."

The plastic ketchup bottle on the table was more than half-full. *Was she planning on drinking it?* I wouldn't have been surprised.

"Sure thing," I said. "Would you like anything to drink? Tomato juice, perhaps?"

She just looked at me, either missing or ignoring my snark. "No."

"Very well. I'll be right back with your meal."

I took her order to the kitchen. Our chef, Bart, looked it over. "So she's back," he said. "The first lady of ketchup."

"Back like a bad cough," I said.

"Some people shouldn't leave their homes," Bart said.

I liked Bart—we all did. He had been with the diner since it opened, when he was young and still had a life, or, at least, dreams. Now he was obese, old, and tired, and lived alone in a Winnebago equally dated and disheveled, on the outskirts of Mistletoe near the town's landfill. The waitresses were the only family—male or female—he had.

As I left the kitchen, a group of men walked in. They were all wearing the same kind of trucking company shirt. I walked over and greeted them, led them to a corner of my section, then got their menus and water. As I passed by Ketchup Lady she said, "How long will it be?"

"Not long," I said.

"Check on my meal before you take that large table's order. I have a busy morning."

I bit my tongue. Literally. I wanted to empty the bottle of ketchup on her head. I went back to the kitchen. To my surprise, Ketchup Lady's order was done.

"Why so fast?" I asked Bart.

"The sooner the ketchup princess eats, the sooner she's gone."

"You're a prince," I said.

"And you're my queen," he replied.

I carried the woman's meal out along with an unopened bottle of ketchup, setting them down on the table in front of her. Ketchup Lady looked up at me with annoyance.

"I said *smothered*."

The omelet was almost drowning in a pool of tomato. "You can add more ketchup yourself if you'd like."

"I didn't come here to make my own food," she said. "That's what I pay you for."

Again I bit down. "Here," I said. I took the opened bottle of ketchup and poured out the rest of its contents onto the plate, pretty much covering everything in a sea of red. I noticed the men at the table next to us were laughing.

"How's that?" I asked.

She looked at it for a moment and then said, "That will do."

I walked back to the kitchen, shaking my head. Fortunately she didn't stay long. As I cleared her table I noticed her plate was clean. Like it had been licked clean. And she left a tip with a note.

Here's your tip. I shouldn't have to ask for more ketchup.

Around a quarter to five, a little before the dinner rush, Loretta came out of her office. "Elle, you've got a phone call. It's Renato," she said with unveiled enmity. Loretta knew Renato. Biblically, I mean. She'd once had a fling with him. I think just about every unmarried woman in Mistletoe had. I was an exception.

I wiped my hands on a dishcloth. "My car must be done." I walked back to her office. The receiver was sitting to the side of the telephone.

"Hello."

"Elle," he said, forgoing his usual terms of endearment. "I have bad news."

My heart panicked. "It cost more than five hundred dollars?"

"No, it is something else. The reason your Fairlane backfired was not because it needed to be tuned up. Your timing belt is going out."

"The timing belt? What does that cost? I mean, it's just a piece of rubber, isn't it? It can't be too much."

"It is like the clutch; it is not the part, it is the labor. The belt is only fifty dollars, but there are a lot of engine parts that need to be removed to replace it."

"Can I drive without it?"

He gasped. "No, *bella mia*. The car will not run without a timing belt. It is more serious than even the clutch."

I groaned, rubbing my eyes with my hand. "How much?"

From the length of his hesitation I knew his answer would be bad. I just didn't anticipate how bad. "Six hundred." He quickly added, "But I will work with you on it. Family discount."

"Six hundred more. With the clutch, that's more than a thousand dollars." I breathed out heavily. "I don't even know if the car's worth that."

"Old cars do not become new," he lamented. "I checked the blue book on your car. It is worth almost two thousand. Maybe you should get a new car."

"But then I'd have a monthly payment . . ."

"Yes, but you have one now anyway. If you sold the car, you could pay off the repairs and use the money toward a monthly payment. It would at least buy you a few months."

I pushed away my panic. "I'll think about it."

"So do you want me to fix it?"

I thought over my predicament. "I can't sell a car that doesn't run," I finally said. "I'll figure something out."

"I'm sorry, *bella*. I wish I could just do the work for you. But it is hard enough keeping the shop open as it is. I got the taxes and payroll. It is killing me."

"I understand. I'd never ask that. When will it be ready?"

"We have to order the belt from Ogden, but William is fast. It should be done by tomorrow night. You'll have it for the weekend."

"Thank you." I hung up and tried not to cry. Maybe I should have. I'm told that crying waitresses make more tips.

CHAPTER

four

*There was a bit of excitement in town today. A man
climbed under his truck. For this town, that's front-page
news. I'm not making fun of this. In larger towns, good
news days tend to be bad days for humans.*
                                            —Elle Sheen's Diary

"I told the kids at school we got a new car, so they
think we're rich," Dylan said the next morning on
the way to school.

"We're not rich," I said. "Why did you tell them that?"

"Albert's family got a new car. His dad's a plumber. He's rich."

I looked over. "Is being rich important to you?"

"We only have old things."

"You're not old. I'm not old."

"You're kind of old."

"Didn't need to hear that today," I said.

"But you're still pretty."

I smiled. "Okay, you've redeemed yourself."

"What does that mean?"

"It means Mama Gator ain't going to eat her young."

I dropped Dylan off, then hurried to the diner. Loretta

was sitting at her desk counting receipts. "Good morning, honey."

"Not so good," I said, stopping at the door to her office. "I need to work more shifts."

Loretta looked up. "You got it, honey. You can start tonight if you like. Cassie just called in sick again. She's got that influenza that's going around. I swear, that girl catches everything. She's a walking petri dish. Trying to earn a little extra for Christmas?"

"Christmas is the least of my worries." I frowned. "I'm pretty sure the universe has conspired to bankrupt me before the year's out."

"Don't flatter yourself, honey. The universe doesn't care that you exist."

"That's . . . so depressing."

Loretta looked at me sympathetically. "I'm sorry, honey. Sometimes it feels like we're running just to stand still."

"I'm running and still going backward."

"Now *that's* depressing," Loretta said. "So I'm going to start putting out the Christmas decorations today."

"Don't do it all yourself," I said. "I want some fun."

"I'll have Bart bring down the boxes when he's got a minute."

I loved it when we decorated. The diner, like the street it was named after, was made for the holiday and wore it well.

"Hey, Elle," Jamie said, invading the back room. "Dennis is here. He's waiting for you."

"Thanks, doll."

I walked through the kitchen toward the front. Bart smiled when he saw me. "Elle."

"Morning, chef-man. Dennis is here. The usual."

"The Dennis usual," he echoed. "Eggs fried hard, side of ham, drizzle of mustard on the side."

"You got it."

Dennis was one of my regulars, as predictable as a snowdrift in December. He was an older gentleman, eighties I guessed, a widower, tall with oversized ears and a massive red nose and silver eyebrows as thick as rope. He wore a gray wool Irish flat cap that I'd never seen off his head, his silver hair peeking out from under it like weeds growing out from under a fence. I had considered that his hair was woven into his hat so he couldn't remove it.

Dennis was sitting in his usual corner booth. He smiled when he saw me. "Hey, Elle."

"Good morning, Dennis."

His brows rose. "But is it?"

"Not really," I said. "But it's a pleasant fiction."

"Indeed," he said. "Got your Christmas shopping done?"

"Haven't even started. How about you?"

He swatted at the air in front of him. "Humbug. I'm too old for that craziness . . ." He shut his menu. I don't even know why he looked at it as he always ordered the same thing. "I'll have the usual with a drizzle of mustard on the side."

"I know. I already put your order in."

"You did, did you?"

"The second Jamie told me you were here. I thought I'd save you some time. Busy man like you."

"Busy man like me," he said, making a low growl. "I'm about as busy as a sloth on sleeping pills. Who knows, I might mix things up on you sometime and order a short stack and hash browns just to keep you on your toes."

"You've come at the same hour, sat in the same booth, and worn the same hat for the last five years. I don't think you'll be mixing things up on me."

"Seven," he said. "You weren't around before that."

"I'll make you a deal. Change the hat and I'll wait for your order."

He grinned. "Fair enough."

Outside the diner came a loud, prolonged honk followed by a staccato chorus of others. The front of the diner was all windows and along with everyone else, I looked out to see what was happening. From what I could see, there was an older model olive-green Ford pickup parked in the street in front of the diner. The driver's-side door was open and, peculiarly, there was no one inside.

"What in tarnation?" Dennis said. "Looks like some fool just ditched his truck in the middle of the road."

Just then Lyle Ferguson, a chunky red-faced man who owned the local hardware store, stormed through the front door of the diner. "Someone call the police."

"What's going on?" Loretta asked, walking out from the kitchen.

"There's a man under that truck," Lyle said.

"He was run over?" Loretta asked.

"No, he just got out and crawled under it."

I walked to the front door and looked out. I could see a man lying on his stomach underneath a truck. "What's he doing?" I asked.

"He's crazy," Lyle said. "He's shouting things in Chinese or something crazy."

"The police are here," I said.

A blue-and-white police car with no siren but lights flashing maneuvered around the stopped cars and pulled up to the curb next to the diner. Two officers got out. I knew both men, as they were diner regulars.

The driver of the police car, a lanky, red-haired officer named Andy, knelt down beside the truck. Then the other officer, Peter, a stocky, thick man with a crew cut, did as well.

Pedestrians stopped on the sidewalk to watch as the drama unfolded. A few drivers, at least those stuck behind the stationary truck, got out of their cars.

"He's under his truck," Dennis said. "That crazy got under his truck."

"That's what I just said," the red-faced man affirmed. "He's lost his mind."

"Probably on drugs," Dennis said. "It's that LSD."

"He should be locked up in an asylum," Lyle said. "Man's mad as a hatter."

I had no idea what was going on, but my heart felt for him. "Maybe he needs some coffee." I poured some coffee into a paper cup and walked out into the cold.

Andy and Peter were still crouched down next to the

truck, which was still idling, the fumes of its exhaust clouding the air around the scene. Like Lyle had said, the man underneath the truck was shouting in a foreign tongue. I didn't understand what he was saying, but I understood the tone—he sounded angry. Or scared.

"Is everything okay?" I asked.

Officer Andy glanced up, surprised to see me. "Stay back, Elle."

The man kept shouting, his voice growing in ferocity.

In spite of the warning, I moved a little closer and crouched down to see who it was. To my surprise, I recognized him. It was William, the new guy at Renato's.

"I know him," I said.

Both officers looked at me.

"You know him?" Andy asked.

I nodded, still looking at the man. Then I said, "William, can you hear me? It's me, Elle. From the shop. Can you hear me? You're going to be okay."

His gaze met mine. He suddenly stopped shouting. The intensity left his face, replaced by a look of confusion.

"I brought you some coffee."

William looked to me like someone who had just woken from a dream. He wiped his eyes. Then he lay on his side and groaned a little, as if recovering from the outburst.

"Are you okay?" I asked.

"Yeah," he said, shielding his eyes.

"Sir," Andy said. "We need you to come out from under the truck."

William looked back over. He still looked a little disoriented. Or maybe embarrassed. "Yes, sir," he said. He slid out from under the truck, sitting on the wet asphalt. The front of his sweatshirt was soaked and dirty. He put his head in his hands.

Andy turned to Peter. "I think we're okay. Go direct traffic."

Peter stood and walked around behind the truck.

Andy turned back to William. "Are you all right?"

"I'm sorry," he said. "I'm not sure what happened."

I moved in closer to William. "I brought you some coffee," I said again. I offered him the cup. "It's black."

William hesitated for a moment, then took the coffee. He drank the entire thing in two gulps, then lowered the cup to his side. "Thank you."

"You're welcome. Would you like me to take the cup?"

He handed it to me.

"We need to get your truck out of here," Andy said to William. "Do you mind if I have Peter drive it?"

"I can move it," he said.

"I'd like my deputy to move it," Andy said.

William rubbed his face. "The keys are inside."

"Thank you," Andy said, though he already knew. The truck was still idling. He turned toward his officer and shouted, "Pete. Move the truck."

"On it," Peter shouted back. As Peter came back around, I said, "Can we get his coat?"

"Grab his coat," Andy said.

Peter grabbed William's thick army-green jacket and handed it to me, then climbed inside the truck.

"Where are you going to take it?" William asked.

"Not far," Andy replied. "Just down to the station. I'll drive you there. We just need to ask you a few questions. Make sure you're all right."

William nodded. Andy stood and offered William his hand. He helped him up. "My car's right here," Andy said.

"Here's your coat," I said.

He took it from me and put it on. "Thank you."

"You're welcome."

William followed Andy to the police car. I just stood there watching as Andy opened the back door and William climbed in. Andy glanced back at me, then got in the driver's seat. The police car drove off followed by William's truck. I walked back inside the diner.

"What was that about?" Loretta asked.

"I honestly don't know," I said.

"It's that LSD," Dennis said. "Kids and drugs these days. I tell you, the world's coming apart at the seams."

CHAPTER

five

Music can open doors our hearts have locked and dead bolted.

—Elle Sheen's Diary

L ater that afternoon I called Renato's. Renato answered the phone.

"Hi, it's Elle."

"*Ciao, bella.*"

"Did you hear what happened with your new guy?" I asked.

"*Si.* William told me. He did not look well so I sent him home. That means your car is not going to be done by tonight."

"I understand."

"Not to worry, *bella.* You can keep the Valiant for the weekend. It is a sexy car."

"Thank you," I said. "Is William okay?"

"I do not know," he said. "But he is a good man. We can hope."

I woke the next morning to eighteen inches of new snow. Dylan wanted me to take him tubing and was upset when I told him that I had to work.

"But you don't work Saturday mornings," he said.

"I know. We just need a little more money right now."

"I hate money," he said.

I hugged him. "So do I. But I wish I had more of it."

Fran watched Dylan while I worked a double. Andy and Peter, the police officers, came in during the dinner shift.

"Hey, Elle," Andy said.

"Hey," I said. "Sit wherever."

"Thanks." Andy always walked stiffly. He once told me that, as a teenager, he had broken his back riding a motorcycle and had never fully recovered.

I grabbed some water glasses and brought them over to the table. "Need a menu?"

"No," Andy said. "We know it by heart."

Peter, who was the more quiet of the two, just shook his head. "I'm good too."

"Wouldn't go that far," Andy said.

"What can I get you boys?" I asked.

Andy said, "I'll have the open-face turkey sandwich smothered in gravy with mashed potatoes, cranberry sauce, and mixed vegetables."

"One Thanksgiving come early," I said. "And what would you like to drink?"

"Ginger beer. And save me a piece of that pecan pie if you still got some."

"We didn't get any today."

"What you got?"

"Apple."

"Apple is good."

"Apple it is."

"I'll have the meatloaf special," Peter said, rubbing a thick hand through his spiky brown hair. "Gravy on top *and* on the smashed potatoes."

"Smash the potatoes," I said. "Did you want some pie?"

"I'll have the apple."

"À la mode?"

"I'll have cheese with it."

"Apple with a chunk of cheddar. Hold the à la mode."

I went back to the kitchen and put in the order. Then, while the chef was cooking, I took a short break to eat my own dinner. I was halfway through my meal when the kitchen bell rang.

"Order up, Elle."

"Thanks, Bart."

"Did you finish your dinner?"

"Do I ever?"

"That's why you're so thin. I'll cook slower next time, let you put some meat on those pretty little bones."

"I've got enough meat on my bones." I grabbed the plates. "And you cook slow enough."

"Oh, you're cold, girl," he said. "Cold as a Mistletoe winter."

"I may be cold, but you're slow." I grinned. "Slow but good."

"That's what all the ladies say," he said.

"You're incorrigible."

I carried the plates out to the police officers. "Here you go, gentlemen."

They both thanked me. Then Andy said, "Hey, I wanted to say, that was really nice of you to take that coffee out to that guy. He really appreciated it. He mentioned it several times."

"So, are you guys friends?" Peter asked.

"No. I just met him a few days ago. He's a mechanic over at Renato's. He's working on my car."

"From under your car to his," Peter said, amusing himself.

"Why did he crawl under his truck?" I asked.

"That's the crazy part," Peter said. He turned to Andy. "You tell it."

Andy cleared his throat. "You know, we see some weird junk on our beat, but I've never seen anything like that. I don't know the term for it, but that guy is a Vietnam vet . . ."

"Shell shock," Peter said. "It happened to a cousin of mine. His brain never really came back from the war. He ended up hanging himself."

Andy nodded. "Apparently he saw a lot of bad stuff over there."

"He told us he lost half his patrol in an ambush," Peter said.

Andy continued, "So yesterday, he was in front of your diner waiting for the light to change when a song came on the radio that, like, triggered him. He suddenly thought he was under attack from the Viet Cong."

Peter shook his head. "Man, you should have seen his face when we got there. It was like staring down the devil. That's something I don't think I'll ever forget. Down at the station he told us he thought we were Viet Cong soldiers. He was shouting at us in Vietnamese."

"I didn't know soldiers had to learn Vietnamese," I said.

"They don't if they don't have to," Andrew said.

"He was a POW for almost four years. He was in that famous Hanoi Hilton," Peter added.

"Oh dear," I said.

"I can't imagine what that would do to your brain," Andy said, shaking his head. "He was with one of the last groups to come home."

My heart was pounding. "You didn't give him a ticket, did you?"

"No. I mean, if I were going by the book, I should have cited him, but sometimes you got to go by the spirit of the law. He fought for our country."

I thought about how harshly I had judged him. "Where's he from?"

"He moved here three weeks ago from Colorado, but originally he's from Indiana."

"What a way to start a new life in a small town," I said.

"It's like they say," Peter said between bites, "wherever you go, there you are."

"Is he okay?" I asked.

"I think so," Andy said. "We took him over to the hospital in Ogden and let someone there check him out. They've got a psychiatric ward there."

"Hopefully they can help," I said.

"That was a tough thing, that war," Peter said, slowly shaking his head. "A lot of those boys never really came back."

Suddenly I teared up. Andy looked over at him. "You idiot."

Peter looked at me. "I'm sorry, Elle. I forgot."

"You *forgot* to plug in your brain this morning," Andy said. "So sorry, Elle. We shouldn't have brought it up."

"It's okay," I said, wiping my eyes. "I asked." I took a deep breath. "I'll stop bothering you boys and let you eat."

"You're never a bother, Elle," Andrew said. "That's why we always come back."

I forced a smile. "You always come back because Loretta's got the best pie in town."

"That too," Andy said, turning back to his plate. "Bless you, Elle."

I started to go, then turned back. "What was the song?"

Andy looked up from his turkey. "The song?"

"The song that set him off."

"Creedence Clearwater Revival," he said. "'Run Through the Jungle.'"

CHAPTER

six

The sermon today was on gratitude. I've always believed that there are none so impoverished as those who deny the blessings of their lives.

—Elle Sheen's Diary

Sunday was the only day I had off all week. It was also my only day to spend with Dylan. The day began as it always did, with me making Dylan waffles with whipped cream and then taking him to church. We were nearing Thanksgiving so the sermon was on gratitude and the power of thankfulness. I was grateful to hear it. I needed to hear it. When you're struggling with lack, it's easy to become obsessed with all you don't have and forget what you do. It was nice to be reminded of all I had to be grateful for.

After church we came home and I made chili and homemade bread, using half the dough for fried scones. (In Utah, the term *scones* is used for what the rest of the world calls fry bread or elephant ears.) My homemaking habits were more than economical. They were reminiscent of my own upbringing. Growing up in Cedar City, my mother made homemade bread every week. At least she would when she wasn't on a bender.

After lunch, Dylan asked if we could go outside and make a snowman. There was enough snow in our little backyard that we could have made an army of them—which Dylan advocated for, but I persuaded him to stop at two: an effigy of each of us.

Afterward we came back inside and, after peeling off layers of snow-covered clothing, we made Christmas cookies. I had a collection of five Christmas cookie cutters: a star, a stocking, an angel, a Christmas tree, and a reindeer, the latter being Dylan's favorite. (Fortunately I had some of those little cinnamon candies to put on the reindeers' noses.)

While waiting for the cookies to cool, I let Dylan eat an unfrosted one and watch TV while I took a forty-five-minute nap—by far my greatest luxury of the week. Then we frosted the cookies and finished our night with our Sunday-evening tradition of lying on my bed and watching *The Wonderful World of Disney* (which, no doubt, would have been much better in color. The last of the networks had switched over to color just a few years earlier).

I looked forward to this, as it was the one time that Dylan would still cuddle with me and let me hold him. I knew it wouldn't always be that way—a fact I mourned. He was my little guy. He was my life. Even with the hardships of those days, I still often thought that I would have loved to freeze that time of Dylan's life. But even then I knew it would be a mistake. To hold the note is to spoil the song.

"Mom, do you think we'll ever get a color TV?" Dylan asked as I put him down for bed.

"That would be nice," I said, which was my standard answer for things I couldn't afford.

"Everyone has a color TV."

"Not everyone. Some people don't even have TVs."

He looked absolutely amazed. "What do they watch?"

I kissed the top of his head. "Life."

❄

Monday morning it was back to the usual grind. The diner's traffic was typical: the local regulars, a half dozen truckers hopping off I-15, the odd salesman stopping by for breakfast.

Dennis came in at his usual time. He was wearing the same hat, of course. In spite of my earlier threat, I didn't put his order in.

"Morning, Elle."

"Good morning, Dennis. How's your day?"

"I'll let you know when it happens," he said. "I'll have the usual. If you didn't already have your guy back there make it."

"No, I waited. A drizzle of mustard."

"A drizzle of mustard."

A few minutes later I brought out his food.

"That was some excitement last week," he said. "Did you ever hear what happened to that guy who was run over by the truck? I looked in the obituaries this morning but there wasn't anyone who had died in a truck-related accident. Had two cancers and maybe a suicide. I had to deduce that, of course. They never state the cause of death if it's a suicide unless you're Hemingway or Marilyn Monroe. And the latter was suspect. You know she was involved with the Kennedys."

Dennis's memory wasn't great. Somewhere over the weekend he must have told himself a different story about the event. Before I could correct him he continued.

"Anyway, the suicide was old Creighton up in Farr West. Certainly not famous or involved with the Kennedys—just not doing well since Lois died. Saw him four weeks ago at the Masonic lodge. He told me that waking was the worst part of his day, next to every other moment."

"I'm sorry to hear that," I said.

Dennis once told me he read the obituaries every day to see if he was in them. If he wasn't, he got dressed.

"He wasn't run over by the truck," I said. "He climbed under it."

Dennis's brow furrowed. "Why would he do that?"

"I guess he wasn't feeling well," I said.

"That makes no sense. Most of the time I don't feel well, but I've never once crawled under my car." He shook his head. "He must still be alive. He wasn't in the obituary."

CHAPTER

seven

Too many people turn to the end of another's story even
before the final chapter has been written.

—Elle Sheen's Diary

I was working a double shift and the only time the diner could afford for me to be gone was between two and four, our slow time. I was eager to get my car back, but by the time the dinner rush ended, Renato's would be closed.

A little before noon I found Loretta in her office. "Loretta, I need to take a break after the lunch rush."

She looked up from her paperwork. "Did the school call?"

"No. I need to pick up my car before the shop closes."

"Fine with me, sugar plum. You hear that, Jamie?" she shouted. "You're pulling double duty this afternoon while Elle gets her car."

"Got it," Jamie said. She was putting on mascara in the bathroom outside Loretta's office. I don't know how Loretta even knew she was there. She had a sixth sense that way.

Before becoming a waitress, Jamie had worked a previous life as a hair stylist, and she saw her body, all six feet of it, as a blank canvas to be painted on—with makeup and hair dye being her preferred media. She wore thick eye shadow the colors of the rainbow with drawn-on eyebrows, overcompensating for what God had neglected.

Truthfully, I wasn't positive what color her hair was, though I guessed it was light brown on its way to gray. Since the day I met her, her hair had been platinum, dishwater blond, strawberry blond, lavender, umber, black, light brunette, chestnut, and flaxen—pretty much the gamut of follicular possibility. Her color du jour was ginger, something that agreed with her.

"Thanks, honey," I said.

"Don't mention it. I'm praying for a miracle healing for your clutch."

I wasn't looking forward to getting my car back. I hated my car. And I was terrified to see the repair bill.

I drove over to Renato's a little before three.

"She's right there," Renato said, pointing toward my car. He handed me the keys with a sheet of yellow paper. "And here is the bill."

I took the paper from him. It hurt to see it. It was for seventy-seven dollars, twenty more than I hoped it would be.

"Seventy-seven?"

"Yes, *signorina*."

I breathed out slowly, then looked into his eyes. "I know you're giving me a good deal, but right now, that's a little steep for my monthly budget. Is it possible we could stretch it out a little more and make the monthly payment in the fifty-dollar range?"

"That is not a payment," Renato said.

I looked at him quizzically. "I don't understand."

"That is the whole bill. *Tutto il conto.*"

It took a moment for me to understand. "But you said it would be more than five hundred just for the clutch. And more for the broken belt."

"That bill is just for parts. There is no charge for labor."

"But . . ." I looked at him with gratitude. "You can't do that."

"Well, I didn't," he said. "William did. He repaired your car on his own time. It took him until four in the morning. You can thank me for the heating bill and him for the labor. *Un bacio* will be fine," he said, turning his cheek to me.

I kissed it, then said, "He fixed my car for free?"

"Except for the cost of parts," Renato said.

I couldn't believe it. "Is he still here?"

"No. He was sick over the weekend so he's taking the day off."

"He was sick while he was working on my car?"

"Very sick. He was coughing like an old tractor. I think he has the influenza," Renato said. "I could barely understand him this morning." He leaned forward even though there was no one else there. "He sounded a little *pazzo.*"

"*Pazzo?*"

"A little delirious. Very sick."

I was speechless. Then I pulled my checkbook from my purse. "I'll pay this now." I wrote a check for seventy-seven dollars and handed it to Renato. "Why did he do that?"

"He said you were kind to him," Renato said.

"All I did was take him a cup of coffee."

"I told you, remember? Do not judge him too harshly."

"I'm sorry," I said. "That was foolish of me." I took a deep breath. "I would like to thank him. Do you know where he lives?"

He scrawled a number on the back of my receipt. "He lives in that apartment building on the end of Noel Street. The one with the *schifoso* yard, just three blocks down from the diner."

"I know the one," I said. "Thank you."

"*Prego, bella.*"

I got in my car and started it. It sounded beautiful. I suddenly began crying. *Why would he do such a thing for me? How could I have misjudged the man so badly?*

CHAPTER

eight

For the last seven years my life has felt like a financial Whack-a-Mole game.

—Elle Sheen's Diary

As I walked back into the diner, Jamie looked me over. "Oh, honey." My eyes must have been red because she hugged me. "I'm so sorry. You'll get through this. I've got a little stashed away, I can help."

Her response only made me cry more. "That's not why I'm crying. He fixed it for free."

"Renato fixed your car for free?" Loretta said, walking into the conversation. "That's a first. That man would charge a baby for diapers."

"It wasn't Renato," I said. "It was the new guy who works for him. William."

"The guy who stopped traffic the other day?" Jamie said. "The one you said was a beast?"

"I'm so sorry I said that. He worked on my car until four in the morning."

"Why would he do that?" Jamie asked.

"I don't know. All I did was take him a cup of coffee."

Loretta shook her head. "That must have been some coffee. Is he single?"

"Is he cute?" Jamie added.

"You two have a one-track mind."

"At least someone's on that track, baby girl," Loretta said. "You're derailed."

"I don't know if he's single."

"Well, you better find out. What did you say to him?"

"I didn't say anything. He wasn't there. Renato said he was sick. He was sick when he worked on my car."

"That's really sweet," Jamie said. "Maybe you should take him some chicken soup."

"That's a good idea," I said.

"I'll donate a crock of chicken noodle to the cause," Loretta said. "And whatever else you want to take him. We got the pecan pie in today. A man fixes your car for free, you better take care of him."

"I'll take him some dinner," I said. "But I don't get off until ten."

"I don't have anything tonight," Loretta said. "You can take off at seven thirty, after the rush."

"Thank you."

"You never answered me," Jamie said. "Is he cute?"

I thought a moment, then said, "Yes. He is."

Loretta nodded. "That always helps."

I was surprised to find myself growing excited about the prospect of seeing William, though, frankly, I had no idea how the encounter would go. I'd seen the man three times. The first time he yelled at my son and then scolded me, the second time he apologized, and the third time he was under a truck hiding from an imaginary enemy. Realistically, I should probably run. But he had blessed my life more than anyone in the last five years and he didn't even know me. Who was this man?

CHAPTER

nine

I went to his apartment anticipating staying for a few minutes, not the night.

                                        —Elle Sheen's Diary

I don't know if it's true of all small towns, but people generally eat early in Mistletoe, and by seven o'clock there were only eight customers in the diner.

Loretta came up behind me as I was filling a drink order. "You can go now, darlin'," she said. "Go see the man." She was carrying a paper bag and a large plastic container with its lid taped down. "I got him a few days' worth of soup." She had gotten more than just soup. She had filled the bag with the morning's pastries, a loaf of hard bread, and some pecan pie. "I threw a few bags of chamomile tea and some packets of sugar in the bottom of the sack. Nothing better for the system when you're sick."

As generous as Loretta was to those in need, I was a little surprised at how fully she'd embraced reaching out to this guy. "That's really kind of you."

"Whatever I can do. Thing is, he helped you, so that

helped me. Otherwise I'd likely have been obliged to give you a raise."

"You were thinking of giving me a raise?"

"Yes, but I came to my senses and talked myself out of it. Now you have a good night and don't go catching anything. I already lost Cassie. I can't afford to have you sick too."

Loretta was peculiar about money. She was simultaneously generous and tightfisted—the kind of person who would give you the shirt off her back and then charge you to wash it.

I carried the food out to my car. It wasn't lost on me that I was driving my car because of him. Instant karma.

I knew the apartment building. Everyone in Mistletoe did, as it was the only one in town. No one I knew had ever lived there, and, from all appearances, its only inhabitants were drifters, strangers, and men in trouble with their wives. The locals just called it "that apartment," but it had a name: the Harrison. It had once been a hotel, named after President William Henry Harrison, whose presidential run lasted a lackluster thirty-one days, as he died of pneumonia after giving his inaugural address in freezing temperatures without a coat. I have no idea why anyone would name a hotel after the man; you would think they would have chosen a president who had accomplished something while in office—or at least had the sense to wear a coat.

The hotel was built more than a hundred years back when Mistletoe was a prosperous mining town. As usually happened, when the veins of ore ran dry, so did the town, leaving a few farmers, homesteaders, and those too old to pick up and start their lives over again. The hotel passed into bankruptcy and eventually it was left to the owner to either tear down or find a way to repurpose it. He chose the latter.

It was dark out, had been for several hours, and the Harrison apartments were near the south end of Noel Street in a bit of a run-down area. In a bigger town this might have been considered dangerous or scary, but this was Mistletoe and its days of newsworthy crime were pretty much past.

There were no lights on this end of the street and a sickle moon lit the area, sparkling off the recently fallen, crystalline-crusted snow.

No one had shoveled the sidewalk in front of the apartments and there was a single set of footprints that led into the building. William's olive-green pickup truck was parked around the side, visible from the street.

I parked my car at the curb out front of the building, got the food out of the back seat, and carried it up the snow-encrusted walkway to the front doors and into the apartment building's dimly lit lobby.

The inside of the building looked as derelict as its exterior. There was a bag of garbage, a bicycle with a flat tire leaning against one of the walls, and a pile of mail on the floor beneath an inset brass mailbox as if the building's residents, past and present, hadn't picked up their mail for a few months.

The place looked like I imagined it might, as if the

owner was absentee and the place's inhabitants were more squatters than renters.

A spiderweb-covered bronze chandelier flickered a little but gave enough illumination to reveal a dirty black-and-white-checkered tile floor. The lobby still looked like it belonged to a hotel. There was a curved stairway with a carved wooden banister leading to a second-story landing with a spindled balustrade.

The base of the stair flared out and, on each side of the stairs, a columnar newel post supported an intricately carved wooden pineapple that had likely once been beautiful but now was chipped and dusty and covered in spiderwebs.

I was startled by a brindled brown-and-black cat that darted across the lobby and disappeared down the darkened hallway.

I took the receipt from my pocket where Renato had written the number of William's apartment. Number 205. I climbed one flight of stairs and walked down the hall to the third door on the right.

Curiously, the door to the apartment was already open a few inches. I set the bag of food down on the floor, then rapped on the door with the back of my hand. There was no answer—at least not from *his* apartment. The door across the hall opened and quickly shut again before I could see who was there.

I rapped again. There was still nothing, though my knocking had opened the door a little more, wide enough to reveal the room's interior, lit by a single yellowish light from a brass floor lamp. I could hear the metallic ticking of a radiator.

"Hello?" I said, then louder, "Is anyone home?"

There was no response.

"William?"

There was a spasm of coughing followed a few moments later by heavy, slow footsteps. A hoarse voice asked, "Who is it?"

I swallowed. "It's Elle. From the diner." Then added, "You fixed my car."

William staggered over to the door. I almost didn't recognize him. He wasn't wearing a shirt; just gray cotton sweatpants that hung loosely from his thin waist. He was lanky and lean in form, but muscular. His right shoulder was covered in a tattoo. He looked sick; his face pale and his hair matted to one side as if he'd been sleeping. His chin was covered in thick stubble. He leaned against the door for support.

"What can I do for you?" he asked, even though he clearly wasn't in a condition to do anything for anyone, including himself.

"I came to thank you," I said, feeling like getting him out of bed was doing more harm than good. "I heard you were sick, so I brought you something to eat." I squatted down and lifted the food. "I brought you some soup. It's still warm."

He coughed, covering his mouth with his forearm. He looked unsteady and in no condition to carry what I'd brought him. "If you don't mind, I'll just put this on your counter."

He nodded slightly. "Thank you." He stepped back from the entrance, though still leaned against the door. I walked past him into the room.

The room smelled dank and musty, old like it was. The apartment still looked like a hotel room, boxy and curtly divided with a small coat closet near the front door. The front room included a small kitchen with a chin-high refrigerator and a small hot plate. The floral wallpaper was faded and torn in places.

What furniture there was looked to be remnants from the hotel days. There was a small table, two chairs, and a low couch upholstered in a threadbare green velvet from the fifties.

On the other side of the apartment, the bedroom door was open and I could see the unmade bed he had just crawled out of. I set the food on the counter.

"Would you like me to pour the soup into a bowl?" I asked.

"No," he said softly. "Thank you."

I sensed that he really just wanted to be left alone. "I'll just leave everything here." I looked back at him. "I'm sorry you're so sick."

"Thank you," he said, the words sounding like they'd taken great effort. He was still leaning against the door like it was holding him up. As I walked back toward him, he put his head down as if he were dizzy. Then he collapsed to the floor with a dull thud.

"William!"

He was unconscious. I put my hand on his forehead. He was burning with fever. I knelt at his side, my hand on his arm. "William," I said softly. "William."

Suddenly his eyelids fluttered open. He gazed at me with a confused expression. "Who are you?"

"I'm Elle. Remember? You fixed my car."

He closed his eyes for a moment, then said, "What are you doing here?"

"I brought you some food. I came to thank you."

He didn't respond.

"We should get you to the hospital," I said. "You're very sick."

"No," he said, squinting with pain. "No hospital. No doctor."

I wasn't sure what to do. Frankly, I wasn't even sure what I was doing. I barely knew this man. Of course, he barely knew me, yet he helped me. I couldn't help but feel somewhat responsible for his sickness, since he'd no doubt gotten sicker working through the night on my car.

"What can I do for you?" I asked.

He closed his eyes and breathed heavily but said nothing. He looked vulnerable and weak, nothing like the powerful, scary man I first encountered at the auto shop.

"Is there someone I can call?"

After a moment he said softly, "There's no one."

The words made my heart hurt. "Don't you have anyone to take care of you?"

"I don't need . . ." He didn't finish the sentence.

I sat there for a moment looking at him. His lips were dry and cracked. I guessed he was dehydrated. "I can help," I said. When he didn't object to my offer I asked, "When was the last time you had something to drink?"

His response came haltingly. "I don't know."

"I'm going to get you some water."

I got up and began looking through his cupboards for a cup. There were only three, two coffee cups and a cheap plastic one. Then I looked inside his refrigerator to see if he had cold water. It was surprisingly bare. There was only a carton of milk, a half-empty jar of Miracle Whip, a small jar of mustard, and an opened package of hot dogs.

I filled the cup with water from the tap and brought it to him. I knelt down next to him and said, "Let me help you drink." I put my hand behind his head. His hair was matted and wet with sweat. "I'm going to help you lift your head."

He groaned a little as I lifted. Then I raised the cup to his lips, supporting the back of his head with my hand. He drank thirstily, though some of the water dribbled down the corner of his mouth, down his stubbled chin. When he had finished the water, he laid his head back. I dabbed the water from his face with my coat sleeve. He shivered.

"You have the chills," I said. "And your fever . . ." I touched his head again. I'd never felt a fever that hot. I wished I had a thermometer but, considering the austerity of his apartment, I doubted he had one. The situation reminded me of a few months back when Dylan was running a fever and I had sat up with him through the night. "Do you have a thermometer?"

"No."

"I'm going to get a cold cloth for your forehead." I looked around his counter and through his drawers until I found a dishtowel. I opened his freezer looking for ice. There was only a frosted package of peas. I wrapped them in the dishcloth and brought them back over to him.

"Tell me if it's too cold."

He coughed again, then closed his eyes. I held the bag of peas to his forehead. I glanced down at my watch. It was past eight. Fran would have already put Dylan to bed. Fran rarely minded staying late, or even spending the night, but I needed to tell her. William shivered again.

"I need to go home and check on my son," I said. "But I'm going to come back. Okay?"

"You don't need to," he said.

"I think I do. Let me help you to your bed. Or do you want to lie here until I get back?"

"My bed."

"I'll help you up." I set my makeshift ice pack to the side and leaned over him. "Put your arms around my neck."

He lifted his arms around my neck locking his fingers together. His breath was warm on my neck. It was strange to think it, but it was the first time in a long time that a man had put his arms around me.

"Let's sit you up first and let you get settled for a moment. I don't want all the blood rushing away from your head." I sat up, and he pulled himself to a sitting position.

A moment later I said, "Tell me when you're ready."

"Ready."

"All right. Up we go."

As I stood, he pushed himself up, using me more for balance than lift. I put my arm around his waist and we walked to the bedroom. He sat down on the side of his bed, then lay back, groaning with the motion. I lifted his legs onto the bed and pulled them a quarter clockwise.

"You just rest. I'll be back in about a half hour."

"Thank you." He rolled his head to the side. For a moment I just looked at him. My heart hurt for his pain but equally for his loneliness. Lately I had obsessed over how hard my life seemed, but I didn't suffer from loneliness. I had friends. I had Dylan. For all I could see, he had no one.

I walked out of his bedroom, shutting the door behind me. I checked his apartment door to make sure it wouldn't lock behind me, shut it, and went down to my car. It had started snowing again, and the windshield was covered with a thin batting of white.

I turned on the windshield wipers and drove down the deserted Noel Street past the diner. The diner was quiet as well and I could see Jamie and Nora inside filling the salt and pepper bottles—one of the things we did before going home each evening.

My duplex was only eight minutes from the diner. I walked in to find Fran sitting on the couch reading a book. She jumped when I walked in.

"I scared you," I said.

"It's the book. It's a suspense novel."

"What is it?"

She held up the book so I could see its cover: *Where Are the Children?*

"That sounds scary. Who wrote it?"

"It's a new writer." She glanced at the cover. "Mary Higgins Clark. She's good."

"And how was Dylan?"

"He went right down," she said. "How was your night?"

"Different than I expected. Would you be okay staying a little longer? I'm taking care of someone."

"Who?"

"Just a friend," I said. "He's new in town. He's sick and doesn't have anyone else."

"No problem," she said. "I can finish the book. Should I spend the night?"

"If you don't mind."

"I don't mind. Is it still snowing out?"

"A little."

"The weatherman said it was going to snow all night. All the more reason to stay put."

"Thank you. I just need to gather a few things."

I looked in on Dylan. He was sleeping soundly, though he'd pulled off most of his covers. I pulled them back up to his chin, kissed his forehead, then went to my room and got a heating pad, a bottle of aspirin, a thermometer, and a couple of washcloths. I grabbed an ice pack and filled it with ice from the freezer, then put it all in a large canvas bag.

"I don't know when I'll be back," I said to Fran on my way out.

"Don't worry about a thing," she said.

"I never do when you're here."

The snow was already coming down heavier. I carried everything out to my car, then drove back to the Harrison. It was nearly ten o'clock when I opened the door to William's apartment. As I walked in I heard a strange guttural noise that sounded more like a growl than a groan. Then I heard William shout out. "No!"

I walked to the door of his bedroom, slowly opening it. "William?"

His eyes were open and he was looking at me, but *not* at me—like he was looking through me. He looked scared.

"Charlies are everywhere, Lieutenant! Let's Zippo it and get out of here."

I didn't know what to do. Was it dangerous for me to be here? He was powerfully built. What if he mistook me for something else?

Sympathy won out. "William, it's just me. Elle. You're in your bedroom. I'm the only one here. Everything's okay."

He stopped, breathed out slowly, then lay back down.

My heart was still racing as I walked to the side of his bed and sat down.

"Hey." I put my hand on his forehead. He was still burning up. I took the thermometer from my bag. "William," I said softly. "I'm going to check your temperature."

He didn't open his eyes but turned back toward me.

"I'm going to put this thermometer under your tongue. Don't bite it." I held his bristled chin as I slid the thermometer between his lips and under his tongue. I held it there for a full minute and then pulled it out. A hundred four degrees. I had spent enough late nights in the ER with Dylan to know this wasn't good.

"You're a hundred and four," I said, setting the thermometer on the windowsill.

"I'm not that old," he said.

In spite of the circumstances, I grinned. "I really should take you to the hospital in Ogden. Would you let me?"

He didn't say anything.

"I can't carry you. Do you think you could walk out to my car?"

"No hospital. No doctors."

I sat there a moment as I thought what to do next. "Well, we need to do something. I brought you some aspirin. Let's at least get that in you."

I went back out to the kitchen and refilled his cup with water, then poured the aspirin into my hand.

"I've got some water and three aspirin. It will help with the fever. Open please."

He opened his mouth and I individually set the pills in.

Then I pressed the cup to his lips. He swallowed the pills with half the cup of water, then lay back.

"I brought you an ice pack," I said.

I set the cup down and pulled the ice pack from my bag. I propped his pillow up so it would hold the pack up to his forehead. It only took a minute for him to fall back asleep, his breathing taking on a calm, slow cadence. "I'm sorry you're so sick," I said. "I won't leave you."

I thought he was asleep—maybe he was—but a single tear rolled down his cheek.

❄

The lights were off, but it wasn't that dark. The moon reflecting off the snow lit the room in a brilliant blue. For nearly an hour I sat on the side of his bed watching him, his face half illuminated like a waning moon. He was so broken. Broken yet beautiful.

At one point he rolled over onto his stomach and the blanket came down from his shoulders. What I saw made my heart jump a little. There were rows of thick scars running vertically down his back. I pulled the blanket down to the small of his back. There were ten-inch scars, more than a dozen of them, raised and angry. I lightly touched one. "What did they do to you?" I asked softly.

Maybe half an hour later I sat down on the floor next to his bed with my back against the wall and closed my eyes but couldn't sleep, which was rare for me.

William got up only once in the night, to use the bathroom. He was disoriented, and I helped him to the toilet. When he came back to bed he said, "Thank you, Nurse," which I think he believed.

I again put the ice pack on his head, then lay down on the floor. I think I fell asleep around one. William woke again around three thirty. He was tossing from side to side. He kept saying, "Don't. Don't. I don't know. I told you." I knelt at his side and gently touched his arm. "You're dreaming. You're okay. You're okay."

His eyes opened and he breathed out heavily, almost panting. Then he caught his breath and looked over at me. Even in the darkness I could see the clearness and intensity of his gaze. This time he was looking directly at me, not at some figment of a nightmare, but into my eyes. Then he said, "I see why he loved you."

I looked at him. "Who?"

He closed his eyes and went back to sleep. I watched him for a moment, then went back to the floor and fell asleep.

I woke a little before seven, the brazen winter sun shining through the blinds, illuminating the room in golden stripes. I didn't know where I was at first, just that my back ached from sleeping on the hard floor. I sat up and yawned. William was still sleeping, lightly snoring.

I leaned over him just to make sure he was asleep, then I put my hand on his forehead. He was still feverish but not as hot as the night before. I pulled the covers up over him and was about to go when he slowly rolled over. His eyes were open. For a moment we just looked at each other.

"You're still here," he said in a raspy voice.

"I said I would be. I need to get my son off to school, then I'll come back." He just stared at me. I leaned over him and touched his forehead and said, "I'll be back."

CHAPTER

ten

Guilt and expediency should not be allowed to coexist in the same mind.

—Elle Sheen's Diary

The night's storm had blanketed my car in nearly a half foot of snow. I got a snow brush from my back seat and scraped off the windows, then drove home.

Fran was wearing one of my sweatshirts. She was in the kitchen making oatmeal.

"Morning, Florence Nightingale," she said.

"Good morning. Is he still asleep?"

"He's taking a shower."

"How'd he sleep?"

"He doesn't even know you were gone. How are you?"

"Exhausted. I slept on the floor."

"That sounds painful." She brought me over a cup of coffee. I took a sip. "Thank you."

"Don't mention it. So who's your sick friend?"

"His name is William. Actually, he's not really a friend. I don't know him very well."

"But you spent the night . . ."

"It's not what you think," I said, drinking my coffee. "I went over to thank him for fixing my car and he was so sick that he passed out. He was all alone. What was I supposed to do?"

"Is he cute?"

"That's not the issue."

"That's always an issue," she said. "So he's not."

"I didn't say that."

Just then Dylan walked into the kitchen. He looked at me curiously—probably because I looked like I had slept in my clothes and my hair was a tangled mane. "Morning, honey."

He didn't say anything about Fran being there. "Hi."

"I've got some oatmeal for you, little man," Fran said.

Dylan walked to the refrigerator and took out a jar of strawberry jam and carried it over to the table.

"Thanks for staying," I said.

"You're welcome. If you're okay, I'll head on home."

"We're okay," I said. "Is it all right if I pay you next Wednesday?"

"You know I'm good," she said. "I left the book on the nightstand if you want to read it."

"You're not going to tell me who dun it?"

She smiled. "Not this time." She walked over and kissed Dylan on the forehead. "Have a good day, handsome little man. I'll see you after school." She looked at me. "Would you like me to pick him up?"

"If you don't mind."

"No problem," she said. "Think you'll be late again?"

"I don't know."

"I'll bring my makeup just in case." She blew me a kiss, then walked out.

I got myself a bowl of oatmeal, put in a spoonful of brown sugar and raisins, then sat down across from Dylan. "How did you sleep?"

Dylan looked up from his bowl. "Good."

"What did you do last night?"

"We did Spirograph. Then we read a book."

"What book?"

"*Andy Buckram's Tin Men*. It's about robots."

"Classic."

His brow fell. "Do you have to work tonight?"

"Yes."

He frowned. "You *always* have to work."

"Someone has to buy the oatmeal," I said. "I don't *always* work."

"It seems like it sometimes."

"I know. It does to me too. But I don't work this Saturday, and on Sunday I don't work until three, so we can go somewhere."

"Where?"

"I don't know. Maybe tubing? If it's not snowing."

"Yeah!" Dylan pumped his fist. "And hot chocolate?"

"It's not really tubing if you don't have hot chocolate after, right?"

He nodded. "Right."

"Now go brush your teeth and pack up your school bag. We need to get going."

Dylan ran off to the bathroom while I put our bowls in the sink to soak. He was right. It felt like I was always working, which wasn't my choice. So why did I have to feel guilty about it too?

He nodded. "Well—"

CHAPTER

eleven

I saw him again today. Twice. Then I ruined everything by opening my mouth. Or maybe it was my heart.
                                                    —Elle Sheen's Diary

I dropped Dylan off at school, then ran by the diner and grabbed some orange juice and a couple of oatmeal muffins.

"You're here early," Loretta said as I walked in.

"I'm just picking up some things for William. I'll put it on my tab."

"William?"

"The soldier."

"Ah. How did that go last night?"

"I ended up spending the night at his place."

Loretta clapped her hands. "There is hope yet!"

"It's not that," I said. "He was so sick that he passed out. I ended up taking care of him all night."

"Well, that's not bad either."

"I'm taking him something for breakfast. I'll be right back."

"Take your time, darlin'. You can't rush love."

"I'm not. I'm rushing breakfast."

I drove back down Noel Street to William's apartment. I

rapped twice on his door and then let myself in. The apartment was still dark and quiet. "I'm back," I said, soft enough not to wake him if he was still sleeping but loud enough not to startle him if he wasn't. Still carrying the juice and muffins, I walked to the door of his bedroom, lightly rapped on it, and then pushed it open. He was in bed but awake.

"Hi," I said.

"You came back."

"I said I would."

"Were you here all night?" he asked.

"Yes."

He looked at me with a curious expression. "Why did you stay?"

"Because you needed me."

He smiled. It was only a slight smile, but it was the first smile I'd seen on him. It was like the sun rising after a cloudy day.

"You have a nice smile," I said.

His smile grew a little more. "Thank you."

"Why did you fix my car?"

"Because you needed me," he said, using my words back at me.

"You have no idea how much you helped." Suddenly the emotion of it caught up with me and my eyes welled up.

"I could say the same. You helped me when I was out in the street."

"All I did was bring you coffee."

"You brought me more than coffee." He slowly shook his head. "You brought me back to reality."

I didn't know what to say to that. After a moment I said, "You must be hungry." I lifted the bag. "I brought you some orange juice and a muffin from the diner." I reached in and took out the muffin. "Here you go."

He peeled the paper off the muffin and hungrily devoured it.

"Would you like the orange juice?"

He nodded and I handed him the cup. He drank it down nearly as fast as he ate the muffin.

"You look a lot better than you did last night," I said.

He set the empty cup down on the stand next to the bed. "What did I look like?"

"Death."

"I felt like death."

"I brought another muffin." I handed it to him.

"Thank you."

He ate while I watched. After he finished the second muffin, he looked up at me. "You're probably wondering why I climbed under the truck."

"I know why," I said. "The police officers who helped you are regulars at the diner. They told me what happened."

"You must think I'm a complete nutcase."

"I think you've been through some very hard things." Then I said softly, "When I was taking care of you, I saw the scars on your back."

I could see that mentioning this brought him pain. "They're kind of hard to miss."

"I'm sorry."

"You're not the one who should be sorry."

I sighed lightly. "I need to go to work." I stood. "I didn't get a chance to get groceries, but I can take a break from work a little later."

"You don't need to do that. You've done enough."

"It's my pleasure. I brought you some soup and bread last night. It's in the refrigerator. You can have that for lunch. Loretta sent you enough food to last a few meals."

"Loretta?"

"She's my boss. She owns the diner."

He nodded. "Please thank her for me."

"I will. There's also pecan pie. I don't know if you like that."

"I love pecan pie," he said. "Back in Indiana I used to buy those little Bama pies, you know the ones?"

"My husband used to like those," I said, softer. "I also brought some chamomile tea. It will help you feel a little better."

"You're making me feel better." For a moment he just looked at me, then he said, "May I ask you something?"

"Of course."

"Why are you being so good to me?"

"Why wouldn't I?"

"I could think of a hundred reasons," he said.

I smiled. "And I can't think of one."

❄

Loretta was still in her office when I got back to the diner. "How's your soldier?"

"He's doing a lot better. He asked me to thank you."

"If you see him again, tell him he's welcome."

"I'll be seeing him again."

"I was hoping as much."

That evening, I left work early again for William; this time so I could stop at the grocery store. I didn't know what he ate, so I bought some basics: oatmeal, bread, butter, milk, eggs, cheese, sliced sandwich meat, and three cans of Campbell's soup. The bill came to almost twenty dollars, but when I thought about the hundreds of dollars he'd saved me it seemed like a small price to pay.

I drove back to his apartment, knocked on the door, and let myself inside, carrying a grocery sack under each arm. His bedroom door was shut. "It's just me," I said.

As I set down the groceries I noticed a saucepan in the sink with residue from the soup I'd left for him. At least he'd been up and eaten something. I quietly opened his bedroom door and looked inside. He was sleeping, so I walked back to the kitchen and put everything away.

"Elle." His voice surprised me, not just because he was awake, but because he had spoken my name. I liked the way he said it.

I walked back to his room and opened the door. "Hi."

"Hey," he said, smiling.

"How are you feeling?"

"Tired, mostly."

"I see you ate something."

"I had some of the soup you brought. It was good."

"Can I make you some chamomile tea?"

He nodded. "I'd like that."

"Do you have a kettle?"

"No. Just the pan I warmed the soup in."

"I can work with that."

William coughed. "I can help."

"No, you stay there. You need rest."

"As you wish," he said.

I smiled. "I wish." I walked back out to the kitchen. I turned on the water in the sink and washed the pan, then filled it halfway with water.

Then I turned on the hot plate and set the pan on its glowing coils; the water hissed as the coils grew bright orange. Once the water was boiling, I opened the cupboard and grabbed one of the coffee cups. One said Winchell's Donuts. The other was a glossy black mug with a white skull and the letters USMC. I chose the donut cup as it seemed more life-affirming and, considering his condition, he needed it. I filled it with hot water and put in one of the teabags.

"Do you like your tea with honey or sugar?"

"Sugar," he said.

I tore open a sugar packet and stirred it in. I let the tea steep for a minute, then took out the teabag and brought the cup to him.

"There you go."

"Thank you." He blew on the drink, then took a sip.

When he set the cup down I reached over and put my hand on his forehead. "You're not as hot as you were. You were a hundred and four last night."

"You took my temperature?"

I nodded. "You don't remember?"

"No." He looked at me for a moment, then said, "From my mouth . . ."

I laughed. "Yes. From your mouth."

"That's good to know. I was kind of vulnerable."

"Yes, you were."

We looked at each other, smiling; was it chemistry?

"I can't stay late tonight," I said. "I've got to get back to my son. But I brought you some groceries."

"Thank you," he said. "How much do I owe you?"

"Nothing," I said.

"Come on. Let me pay you."

"After what you did, it would be embarrassing for me to take your money."

"It would be embarrassing for me to take a handout from a single mother."

I nodded. "Then you're going to have to be embarrassed."

He looked at me gratefully. "Thank you."

"You're welcome."

"You don't have to stay here. You've wasted enough time on me."

I looked at him for a moment then, to my own surprise, said, "I've enjoyed being with you."

"It's mutual," he said. He sipped his tea and then asked, "Do you know what day it is?"

"It's November eighteenth."

"What day of the week?"

"Tuesday."

He looked confused. "I think I missed a few days."

"No doubt." I smiled. "Well, I better go." I started to leave, then stopped and turned back.

"Last night you said something peculiar."

"Yes?"

"You said, 'I see why he loved you.'"

He was quiet a moment, then shook his head. "I must have been delirious."

"You were very sick." I breathed out. "Well, I better run." I looked at him again and then said, "Would you like to do something sometime, maybe get something to eat?"

"Thank you. That's a really kind offer, but . . ." He looked me in the eyes. "Could I say no?"

I flushed with embarrassment. "Of course. I didn't mean anything, I just . . ." I wasn't sure how to finish the sentence.

"I really appreciate all you've done for me."

"It's nothing compared to what you've done for me," I returned. "Besides, I'm partially to blame for you being sick. If my car wasn't broken down, you wouldn't have been working all night in the cold. You could have died from exposure." I forced a grin. "Like the guy they named this apartment building after."

"Harrison," he said. "But I'm not dead yet."

The moment fell into awkward silence. Finally I said, "Well, I better go. If I can do anything for you . . ."

"I hope I didn't offend you."

"No," I said. "You didn't." Then I added, "Maybe bruised my ego a little."

He grinned. "Then I'm sorry for the bruises."

"Forgiven," I said. "I'll see you around." I walked out of his apartment. As I descended the stairs, my eyes welled up in embarrassment. It seemed that I was undesirable to everyone but old men and lonely truck drivers. My heart ached as I drove home to take care of my son.

CHAPTER

twelve

I guess he changed his mind about me. I wonder what happened.

—Elle Sheen's Diary

The next morning at work Jamie asked, "How's your patient?"

"He's fine," I said.

"That wasn't very convincing."

"He's not my patient anymore. He's better."

"But you'll still be seeing him?"

"Apparently not."

"What do you mean?"

"I asked him if he'd like to go out sometime. He turned me down."

"Loser," she said, shaking her head.

"He's not a loser," I said.

She looked at me with surprise. "Oh my. You're defending him. Feelings, perhaps?"

"No," I said. "There are no feelings."

"Really?" she said. "So he's just another fish in the sea?"

"I don't have a sea," I said. "I don't have any bait and I'm too tired to fish. I just want to get back to work."

"Oh, you got bait, girl," she said after me. "You just forgot how to use it."

It was a long day. I operated on little enough sleep as it was, but that late night caring for William had finally caught up to me. It was after the dinner rush when Jamie came to the breakroom to find me. "Elle, you've got to come out and see who just walked in."

"Who now?" I asked.

I followed her out. She pointed toward the door. "That's him, right?"

William was standing inside the door next to the PLEASE WAIT TO BE SEATED sign. He still looked a little pale. I admit it was a little painful to see him. "Yes, that's him."

"He's gorgeous."

"Then you should ask him out," I said. "Maybe he won't turn you down."

"No, he's yours," Jamie said. "Go get him."

I took a deep breath, then walked over to him. He smiled when he saw me.

"Dinner for one?" I asked, trying not to sound hurt or distant and probably failing at both.

"It's just me," he said. "As usual."

"You can sit wherever."

He looked around, then said, "Where are you serving?"

"That section," I said, gesturing to my zone with a

menu, which I handed to him. "You can seat yourself. I'll get you some water."

"Thank you."

A moment later I brought him a glass. "Do you know what you want?"

"A chili cheeseburger and fries."

"And to drink?"

"A Dr Pepper."

"Anything else?"

"I would like to apologize."

I looked up from my pad. "For what?"

"You asked if I wanted to do something sometime, and I said no."

It hurt just hearing it again. "Don't worry about it."

"I haven't stopped worrying about it since you left. I came to see if I could take you out to dinner."

"Why do I feel like you're doing this out of pity?"

"Because I am," he said.

"Oh, really?" I said.

"Not for you," he said quickly. "For myself. Any man who would turn down an offer like that from a beautiful woman like you is pretty pitiable. Or maybe he was just a recluse who was out of his head recovering from an illness."

"You were pretty sick," I said.

"Delirious," he said. "Totally out of my head."

"I might be able to cut you a little slack—being sick and all."

He grinned. "You are as merciful as you are beautiful."

I smiled.

"Are you busy tomorrow night?"

"I'm off," I said. "But I'll need to find a sitter for Dylan. Can I call you?"

"I don't have a phone at my apartment, but you can call me at Renato's."

"You're already back at work?"

"I start back tomorrow. Renato needs the help. He came over this morning to see if I had a pulse."

"Apology aside, do you still want the food?"

"A man's got to eat."

"Yes, he does."

Back in the kitchen Jamie said, "How did it go?"

"He came to apologize and ask me out."

"Did you accept?"

"Of course."

Jamie smiled. "Smart girl."

William didn't stay long. He wolfed down his burger and was gone. He left me a ten-dollar bill for a four-dollar meal.

CHAPTER

thirteen

I'm so scared. It's been more than nine years since I went out on a date. Back then I was childless. The playing board has changed substantially, but the pawn is still vulnerable.

—Elle Sheen's Diary

A few minutes after he left, I called Fran to see if she could watch Dylan. As usual, she was happy to help.

The next morning I called William at Renato's. It took him a while to come to the phone.

"Sorry. I was under a car."

"Again?" I said.

He laughed. "It's getting to be a habit."

"So, I got a sitter."

"That's good news," he said happily. "Can I pick you up at six?"

"Six is good."

"Is there anyplace in particular you'd like to eat?"

"Anyplace but the diner."

He laughed again. "Fair enough. Do you like Italian food?"

"I love Italian food."

"Renato recommended a place in Ogden. DiSera's Italian. Have you been there?"

"No, but I've heard it's good."

"I'll make reservations," he said. "I'll see you at six."

"See you then."

I hung up. It had been years since I'd been out on a date. Let's be honest—it had been years since I'd been out anywhere. I couldn't wait.

CHAPTER

fourteen

William took me to a fancy Italian restaurant. He
listened too well and I talked too much. In other words, I
still have no idea who he is.

—Elle Sheen's Diary

I finished work that day at two. On my way out, Loretta stopped me at the back door.

"I hear you have a date," she said. "With the soldier."

"Word spreads fast."

"It's a small town. Where are you going on this date?"

"DiSera's. In Ogden."

"Oh, he's a big spender," she said. "That's pricey."

"You've been there?"

"Many times. Renato loves that place. Their lasagna is delicious, as is their gnocchi and sage-butter spaghetti."

"You're making my mouth water."

"Which is what I hope your date does for you."

"You're incorrigible."

"Yes, I am. I was hoping it might rub off on you."

I drove home, showered again so I didn't smell like coffee and cigarettes, then went through my closet looking for something to wear. I didn't have many things to dress up in. The life I was living didn't require anything. I ended up in a high-necked blouse with ruffles on the cuffs that Loretta had given me the previous Christmas and a long denim skirt.

Fran arrived at a quarter to six. "You look nice," she said. "Love the blouse. Where are you going?"

"I'm going out on a date," I said proudly.

She looked at me like I was speaking a foreign language. "A date?"

"Try not to look too surprised."

"Who's the lucky man?"

"William," I said. "He's the one I was taking care of earlier this week."

"Ah," she said.

"What does that 'Ah' mean?"

"It means that I wondered if there was a little flame there. I mean, you did spend the night."

"I didn't 'spend the night.' He was sick," I said. "It's just a first date."

Just then Dylan came out of his room. "Where are you going, Mama?"

"I'm going out to dinner with a friend."

"Can I go?"

"No, not this time, buddy."

He looked puzzled. "How come?"

I realized that this had to be strange for him. Outside of work, I rarely, if ever, went anywhere without him. "Sometimes moms need time for themselves."

"How come?"

"They just do," I said.

Thankfully, Fran interjected. "Dylan, I thought you were going to watch TV with me."

"I want to go with my mom."

"We can watch *The Waltons*."

"I don't want to watch *The Waltons*."

"How about *The Six Million Dollar Man*?"

"All right," he said.

A few minutes later the doorbell rang.

"That's him," I said. "I don't know when I'll be home. We're going to dinner in Ogden."

"The big city," she said. "What time do you want Dylan in bed?"

"He can stay up late. Maybe nine."

"Do you want me to stay the night? Just in case?"

"In case of what?" I said. I opened the door. William stood in the doorway. He was dressed in bell-bottomed jeans and a knit sweater. His hair was nicely combed and he was clean-shaven.

"You look nice," he said.

"Thank you, I was thinking the same about you. I just need to get my coat. Come in."

As I walked over to the closet, Fran approached William.

"I'm Fran," she said, looking a little too interested.

"I'm William. It's nice to meet you. Thanks for babysitting."

"It's cool," she said.

"All right," I said, walking between them. "I'm ready." I looked around. "Dylan? Where are you?"

Dylan was hiding behind the kitchen table. I forgot that Dylan and William had unresolved history.

"Dylan, come here."

"No."

"Dylan," I said more forcefully.

William raised his hand. "It's okay." He walked into the kitchen, crouching down a couple of yards from Dylan. "Dylan, my name is William. We got off to a rocky start, so I brought you something. It's a peace offering."

"What's that?"

"A peace offering is something you bring someone to say you're sorry. In this case, it's a candy bar." He brought a Hershey's Chocolate bar from his jacket. "Do you like chocolate?"

Dylan nodded.

William turned to me. "Is this okay?"

"It's too late now," I said. "He's seen the goods."

He smiled, then turned back. He handed Dylan the candy bar. "I'm sorry I yelled at you. I promise I won't do that again."

Dylan took the chocolate. "It's okay."

William put out his hand. "Then we're cool?"

"We're cool," Dylan said, taking his hand.

"All right," William said, standing. "Big relief."

"Since you boys have it together," I said, "can we go?"

"Have a good time," Fran said to William.

Then she leaned in and whispered, "He's cute."

"Maybe you should sleep over," I said. I put on my coat and walked out with William into the cold.

"I'm in the Cadillac," he said, motioning to his green pickup.

"I remember."

He opened the door for me and helped me in, then he walked around and climbed in the other side. There was a Little Trees air freshener hanging from the mirror.

"I'm sorry, it smells like motor oil in here. I bring my work home with me."

"You work on cars at home?"

"I meant the oil," he said. He started the truck and pulled out into the road.

"By the way, good job with Dylan," I said. "You won him over."

"The magic of chocolate. Does wonders with kids."

"I've got news for you. It's not just kids. It's pretty much catnip for women."

He looked over and smiled. "That's good to know."

❄

DiSera's was one of the nicest restaurants in Ogden, evidenced by the full parking lot. I followed William into the crowded lobby, passing several people grumbling about the long wait.

William walked up to the hostess, who, understandably, looked a little frantic.

"May I help you?" she asked.

"We have reservations for seven," William said. "It's under Smith."

She looked at her guest book, then looked back up. "William Smith for two?"

"Yes, ma'am."

"It will just be a few moments while they clear the table, Mr. Smith for two."

"Thank you."

I looked around the dimly lit restaurant. Outside of the diner, I hadn't been in any restaurant for several years. I watched the waiters and waitresses scurrying about with a kind of shared empathy, wondering what it would be like to work in an environment where people dressed up to eat.

"Follow me, please," the hostess said.

William motioned for me to go first and I followed the hostess to a candlelit table in the corner of the main dining room. William pulled out the chair for me and I sat down. The hostess unrolled our napkins and handed us menus in faux leather frames.

"Charlotte will be right with you," she said.

William looked at me and smiled. "Does it feel different being on the other side of the menu?"

"It feels different sitting down to cloth napkins." I looked over the menu. The prices of the meals were triple those at the diner. I instinctively began looking for the cheapest item.

"I hear the lasagna is good," he said.

"I've heard that too," I said. "It's expensive. Everything on the menu is expensive."

"You're worth it," he answered.

I smiled at him. "I may be, but you don't know that."

"Maybe I do," he said. "You're easily the best nurse I've ever had."

"Maybe I missed my calling in life."

"Would you like some wine?" he asked.

"Yes." I loved wine but, with the exception of Loretta's Christmas party, I hadn't had any in two years. "I love red wine."

"They have some excellent Chiantis," he said.

"You've been here before?" I asked.

William shook his head. "No. Renato told me. He speaks reverently of this place. I think food is akin to religion in Italy."

Our waitress came with a basket of breadsticks. "May I take your order?"

"Please," William said, deferring to me.

I ordered the lasagna. William ordered the spaghetti with clams and requested a wine list. A few minutes later the restaurant's sommelier came out with their list and his recommendations. He returned with a bottle of a Ruffino Chianti Classico and poured our glasses.

I sipped the wine. "This is really nice. I don't want to know how much it cost."

"You don't need to worry about that. We're celebrating."

"What are we celebrating?"

"Whatever we want," he said.

"Maybe I should get a job here," I said. "Getting tips on this menu would change my world."

"How much of your income is in tips?"

"Most of it. It's not a lot, obviously."

We both took a drink of wine. "That is good," he said.

"Heavenly," I said.

He set down his glass. "Were you born in Mistletoe?"

"No. I'm from Cedar City."

"Where's that?"

"It's a town in southern Utah. It's not as small as Mistletoe. I didn't even know Mistletoe existed until the day I arrived there. It's one of those towns you drive past on the way to somewhere else."

"How did you end up there?"

"Now that's a story."

"I'm up for a story," he said.

"It may cost you another drink," I said.

William smiled as he refilled my glass.

I took another sip of wine. "So, how I ended up in Mistletoe. Basically, I ran away from home. At least what was left of it. My parents disowned me or maybe I disowned them. It went both ways."

"What happened?"

"I married someone they didn't want me to marry."

"They didn't like him?"

"They never met him," I said. "He was black."

He nodded knowingly. "Where did you meet?"

"In school. We fell in love. But I knew my parents would never approve of me marrying a black man, so after a year of dating, we were secretly married and living a double life.

"I wish we had been more open, but neither of us had any money. Finally, he dropped out of school to work." I paused. "That's when he was drafted into the war." I took a drink, then a second.

"He didn't believe in the war. He said he had some friends moving to Canada to avoid the draft, but I wasn't going to do that. I was still a small-town girl. I didn't think there was life outside Cedar City, let alone America. I couldn't leave my friends and family." I sighed heavily. "If only I'd known how things would turn out. I lost my family *and* him." I took another drink. William just looked at me sympathetically. I was drinking too much. It certainly loosened my tongue.

"The thing is, my family bleeds red, white, and blue. My great-grandfather served in World War I as a general, my grandfather was a colonel in World War II, and my father served in the Korean War. I told my husband that if we ever hoped to have my father accept us, he'd have to serve. So he did, for me." My eyes suddenly moistened. "I asked too much. He never came back."

"I'm sorry."

"Me too," I said. I took another drink of wine. "But he left me something. We didn't know it at the time he was deployed, but I was pregnant. My parents, of course, were apoplectic. They thought I was an unmarried pregnant woman."

"You didn't correct them?"

"Not at first. I knew that the truth, to them, would be worse. When they finally learned that I was married and that my baby would be black . . ." I shook my head. "Let's just say they weren't real pleased.

"I thought they'd change their mind after Dylan was

born. I thought, who could reject a baby? But they did. About six months later we got in a big fight. My mother said he wasn't their grandson and never would be. I remember looking at my father, waiting for him to come to my defense, but he said nothing. I think that silence was worse than my mother's rejection." I breathed out. "That pretty much destroyed any chance of reconciliation. I told them that if they disowned their own grandson, then I was disowning them. That's when I left. I had a hundred and fifty dollars and the Fairlane my grandfather had given me.

"Unfortunately, I pretty much left without a plan. I drove north, looking for a job. I couldn't find anything. I wasn't exactly a stellar candidate—a single college dropout with a six-month-old baby. Dylan and I slept in the back seat of the car. After a week I was desperate. I was exhausted and almost out of money.

"That's when I found Mistletoe. I was driving at night. It was snowing so hard, I was afraid I'd drive off the interstate. Then I saw this light ahead. It was the diner. I was down to my last few dollars and gas. I was just praying that something would work out.

"I carried Dylan inside the diner. When I walked in, the place was almost deserted. There were Loretta, Jamie, and a couple of truckers. One of the truckers spun around in his chair, looked me over, and said, 'Well look what the storm blew in.'

"Loretta was on him like sesame seeds on a bun. She got in his face and said, 'You say one more word like that and that's the last meal you'll eat at my place. You got me?'

"The man backed down like a scolded schoolboy. He said, 'Yes, ma'am.'

"Then Loretta came up to me and said, 'What's his name, darlin'?' I told her. She took Dylan from me and then said, 'Sit down, sweetie, before you fall down. What do you want to eat?' I said, 'Just some coffee and toast. I don't have much money.' She said, 'You're in luck, girl. We've got a special on dinner tonight. It's free ninety-nine.' She kept bringing me food; then, after I was done eating, she asked where I was spending the night. I said, 'We've been sleeping in the car.' She said, 'That's no place for a baby. Where are you headed?' I said, 'Wherever the road takes us.' She said, 'Well, honey, it's taken you here. And I have a room in back you can stay in. Lord knows we've got plenty to eat.'"

"What a good woman," William said.

"Yes, she is." I smiled sadly. "She saved my life. I found out later that her only son had committed suicide just two months earlier and she was still raw."

William seemed to process this. Then he asked, "She offered you a job?"

"No, she never really hired me. It more or less just happened. At first I started helping out just to thank her. I did dishes, helped in the kitchen, then I started pouring water and bussing tables for the waitresses. They started sharing their tips.

"The other waitresses were sweet as can be. It was like Dylan had a plethora of mothers. They helped watch Dylan and I helped them all I could. I don't know where I'd be without them."

"What about your parents?"

"I haven't talked to them since I left home. They're pretty much dead to me."

"What was your relationship like before you left?"

His question surprised me. "It was good, once. My father and I used to be really close. When I was sixteen, I didn't get asked to my first prom. That night I was in bed, crying. He knocked on my door and then came in. He said, 'Why aren't you dressed? We have reservations.' He had bought me a corsage. He took me out to dinner and dancing." I looked down, the memory freshly burning. "We used to be close."

"What about your mother?"

"We never really got along. My mother drank a lot. She really struggled, but the demon owned her. I used to ask my father why he stayed with her, but he just said, 'A soldier never leaves his post.'"

I swished what was left of the wine in my glass. "You have to give him credit. He was loyal. At least to her. Not so much to me. Maybe that's what makes it hurt so much."

"I'm really sorry," he said.

"So here I am. I always thought, once my husband gets back, everything will change. I might even finish school."

"What did you want to do?"

"I wanted to be a writer."

"Like . . . books?"

I nodded.

"Maybe someday I'll write my story."

"I'd read it," he said.

"Thanks. I'll autograph it for you." I breathed out. "Enough about me. What about you? What brings you to Mistletoe?"

"My truck," he said.

"Something brought you here," I said. "No one arrives in Mistletoe by accident."

"I'm sure that's true," he said. He took a drink of wine, looked at me, then said, "I figured it was a nice place to die."

I wasn't sure if he was joking or how to respond, but the moment was interrupted by our waitress. "Sorry for the wait, here is your Spaghetti alle Vongole," she said, setting the plate in front of William. "And your lasagna, ma'am. Would you like some Parmesan cheese?"

"Yes, please."

The waitress grated cheese over my pasta. "And you, sir?"

He raised a hand. "No, thank you. I have it on good authority that Italians never put cheese on seafood."

"Very well," she said. "*Buon appetito.*" She walked away.

I picked up the conversation. "So, you won't tell me what brought you here, maybe you'll tell me where you came from."

"Denver. Most recently."

"What did you do there?"

"I worked at a car dealership for a while, maintaining cars."

"Did you always want to be an auto mechanic?"

"It was more something I did than aspire to. I was raised in Fort Wayne, Indiana. I guess being that close to the

Indianapolis Speedway, cars got into my blood. I always wanted to race cars."

"But you moved to Denver?"

"After the war . . ." He hesitated. "Things changed."

We ate a moment in silence. Loretta was right; the lasagna was delicious.

William took another drink of wine, then said, "The thing about war is, everything you think you know about humanity, or about yourself, is challenged. Especially in a conflict like Vietnam." He looked at me over his glass. "Did you know that Vietnam wasn't even a war? It was never approved by Congress, so technically it's considered a conflict." He shook his head. "Semantics and politics. When bullets are flying at you, it doesn't matter what you call it."

"Were you drafted?"

"Sort of," he said.

"What does that mean?"

"If I tell you, you're going to totally wonder what you're doing with me."

I smiled. "I already am."

"Then I have nothing to lose," he said, grinning lightly. "So I'm what they call a two-or-ten."

"Two or ten?"

"The judge pounded his gavel and gave me a choice: two years in 'Nam or ten years in prison. I chose the former."

"What did you do?"

"Got in with the wrong crowd, mostly. I ended up

spending time in prison anyway—the Hanoi Hilton. I would have done better at home." His voice fell an octave. "At least they're not allowed to torture you in US prisons."

I let his words settle. "You served your country. That was an honorable thing."

"I wish it were that simple," he said. "I risked my life and had no idea what I was fighting for—a corrupt dictatorship that represented almost everything we're fighting against?" He took another drink of wine. "Needless to say, I'm pretty much a hot mess."

I had never before heard the term but liked it. "A hot mess. That sums us both up."

"The difference between you and me is that you can't afford chaos," he said.

"Why do you say that?"

"Because you care about your son more than yourself," he said. "You're a good person."

"So are you," I said.

He looked at me skeptically. "Now that's the wine talking."

I reached over and touched his hand. "No, it's my gratitude talking. What you did for me . . . Aside from Loretta, no one has ever helped me like that. Dylan and I are barely getting by. It would have taken me years to pay off that debt. You didn't even know me and yet you helped us. Hot mess or not, you have a good heart."

He took another drink and said nothing. He went to pour more wine into my glass but I put my hand over it. "That's enough. Are you trying to get me tipsy?"

"I'm just trying to make you feel good."

I looked at him for a moment, then said, "It's been a long time since anyone has tried to do that."

"Am I succeeding?"

I smiled. "Spectacularly."

We split a piece of tiramisu and, I confess, I had another glass of wine. It was the most relaxed I had felt in years.

Around nine o'clock he asked, "What time do you need to be back?"

"It doesn't matter. My sitter is spending the night."

"Can I show you something?"

"Sure."

"Come with me."

It was late and the restaurant was only half-full as we left the parking lot. William drove us about six miles up alongside a small canyon I'd never been to before. The canyon road was narrow and snow-packed. About four miles up the canyon he stopped his truck next to a large snowbank. It was dark, and the granite walls were mostly concealed by snow-frosted pines whose tops disappeared into the darkness of night.

"Is this it?" I asked.

"No. It's down that road a quarter mile. But there's more snow than I thought there'd be. I don't want to get the truck stuck. And you're not dressed for walking in snow."

"What is it that you wanted to show me?"

"It's just a place," he said.

"What kind of place?"

He turned to me. "A peaceful place."

I looked at him for a moment and then said, "I want to see it."

"You'll get cold. Especially your feet."

"It's a small price to pay for peace."

"Are you sure?"

I nodded. "I'm sure."

He got out of the truck and walked around to my door and opened it and helped me down. He took my hand. "If it gets too cold, just tell me and we'll come back."

"It's a deal."

Hiking through the snow was harder than I expected. The snow was up to our knees in places as we trudged along a narrow, uncleared path surrounded on both sides by columnar trees, white and frozen, lining the path like marble pillars. The cold air froze our breath in front of us.

Suddenly we came to a clearing that overlooked the valley below. William stopped. "This is it."

"Oh my," I said. In front of us was a waterfall, the exterior draped in an intricate lacework of ice. The sound of laughing, rushing water escaped the ice veil and fell below into a river whose banks were piled with snow. Everything around us was white, crystal, and blue, lit by a full moon that hung naked in the winter air.

"They call this Lace Veil Falls," he said.

"It's beautiful," I said, my voice muffled in the blanket of winter that surrounded us. I looked at him. "How did you find this place?"

"I found it the day after I moved to Mistletoe," he said. "I sat up here one night and just looked out over the valley."

"In the cold?" I asked.

"In the cold . . ."

His words trailed off in silence.

After a while I said to him, "Thank you for sharing this with me."

"You're welcome," he said softly. He turned and looked at me. I had my arms crossed at my chest and I was shivering.

"You're freezing."

"I'm a little cold."

"Let's get you back." We walked about twenty yards when he looked at me and said, "Your feet must be frozen."

"It's not much farther," I said.

"I can carry you."

"Really, you don't have to . . ."

He reached down and lifted me, his muscular arms embracing me. "This is better."

I was thinking the same thing. It felt good to be in his arms as he effortlessly carried me through the thick powder. He carried me all the way to his truck, set me down, and opened the door, then lifted me in. It was the most romantic thing I'd experienced in years. When he got back in the truck he was quiet. Then I noticed that his eyes were wet.

"What is it?" I asked.

He didn't look at me. He just started his truck and then reached over and turned on the heater, turning the vent toward me.

"What is it?" I asked again.

"It's nothing."

I reached over and touched his arm. "Something just happened, didn't it?"

He took a deep breath, then said, "Thank you for sharing that with me. I wanted to share that with someone."

We drove in silence back to my duplex. It was almost midnight when we arrived. We parked at the curb, and William walked me to the door.

"Thank you for tonight," I said. "It was really nice talking to you."

"Would you like to go out again?"

"I would love to."

He thought a moment, then said, "Is tomorrow too soon?"

I was happy that he was so eager. "I'd love to but I work tomorrow night."

"How about Saturday?"

"I work at night, but during the day I could do something." I caught myself. "I'm sorry . . . I promised Dylan I'd take him tubing."

"We can do that," he said.

"You want to go tubing with us?"

"It sounds fun. As long as you wear the shoes for it."

I smiled. "I wasn't going to wear boots to a nice restaurant."

"And the evening was the better for it," he said. "So, as far as the tubing goes, I have inner tubes and an air compressor at the shop. The tubes will fit better in the back of my truck than in your Fairlane."

"You talked me into it," I said.

"What time would you like to go?"

"Is nine good?"

"It's good for me."

Our words gone, we stood there quietly looking at each other. I wondered if he was going to kiss me. I was hoping he would. Instead he put out his hand. "Thank you."

I took his hand. "You're welcome. Good night."

I opened the door and stepped inside. I couldn't wait to see him again.

CHAPTER

fifteen

Why is it that the people with the smallest minds have the biggest mouths?

—Elle Sheen's Diary

"How did the date go?" Jamie asked the next morning, pouring cream into a coffee cup.

I must have smiled. It was kind of automatic.

"That good, huh?"

"He was really sweet. And the restaurant was amazing."

"So, is there a sequel to this romance?"

"I wouldn't call it a romance."

"What would you call it?"

I smiled wider. "Fun."

"That's even better," she said. "So when are you seeing him again?"

"We're going tubing with Dylan tomorrow."

"Getting in with the son. That's fast."

"It's not that. He asked me out and I'd already made plans with Dylan, so he offered to come along."

"Sounds like romance to me," Loretta said, walking past us to the kitchen.

"That woman should work for the CIA," Jamie said.

"Thought about it," she shouted back.

About an hour into my shift I got a call from Fran. She sounded awful. "Elle, I'm so sorry. I've come down with something. I'm so sick I had to miss school."

"What do you have?"

"Everything. I've got a sore throat, chills, fever. I could feel it coming on last night. I don't think I should watch Dylan."

I wondered if I passed it on to her from William. "I'm sorry. I'll pick up Dylan and bring him here."

"Are you sure?"

"Of course. You get some rest. Get better."

"How was your date last night?"

"It was nice," I said. "You take care of yourself. I need you."

"I need you too. Bye."

It wasn't the first time I had to bring Dylan with me to the diner. Fortunately, Loretta was always good about it. In fact, I think she enjoyed it.

A little after two o'clock I picked Dylan up from school, stopped by home to get him something to do, then came back to work. Loretta was in her office when we walked through the back door.

"I'm sorry, Loretta. Fran's sick, so I had to get Dylan."

She smiled at Dylan. "Lucky us," she said. "How's my handsome man?"

"Good, Ms. Loretta. Can I have a hot chocolate?"

"Of course you can. With whipped cream?"

"Yes, ma'am."

"You have such nice manners that I'm going to get you a donut to go with that."

"Just sugar him up," I said.

"Someone's got to," Loretta said.

I said to Dylan, "Hang up your coat, then take your bag out to the corner table. You can do your Spirograph. Just don't bother anybody."

"I won't." He hung up his coat and walked out to the table in the farthest corner of the dining room. There's a reason I had told him not to bother anyone. Dylan was always well behaved, but he was naturally curious as well as a consummate socialite and liked talking to strangers. And, frankly, now and then there were people in the diner I didn't really want him talking to.

I took him his hot chocolate and donut, then went back to work.

Around six o'clock I was taking an order when I noticed William walk through the front door. He was wearing a green army jacket with his hands deep in his pockets. I waved to him and he smiled and tipped his head. I finished taking the table's order and then walked over to him.

"Hi. What brings you here?"

"I just thought I'd come get something to eat."

"Oh," I said. "Then your being here has nothing to do with me?"

He grinned "Maybe a little."

I felt like a smile was commandeering my face. "I had such a good time last night."

"Me too," he said. "You're pretty good company. Sorry about the snow hike."

"Frostbite aside, it was my favorite part of the night," I said. "I'm serving this side, so just grab a table. Dylan's back there. Why don't you go on back and say hello?"

"Dylan's here?"

I nodded. "My sitter called in sick."

"I won't be eating alone after all," he said. He headed back toward Dylan. Dylan looked up with a big smile which, of course, translated to an even larger smile on my face.

A few minutes later I took William's order. It was interesting watching Dylan respond to being with him. He ordered the same thing William did—a toasted tuna salad sandwich with coleslaw and fries. And a large dill pickle. I don't think I'd ever seen Dylan eat a pickle before.

A few minutes later Andy walked in. He was in uniform but alone this time. I sat him just a few tables from William before wondering if, considering their last encounter, that was such a great idea. As I walked back to the kitchen I noticed that William got up and walked over to Andy's table and shook his hand.

It was about twenty minutes later when I was just coming back to the kitchen after serving Dylan and William that Jamie said, "Sorry, baby, she's baaaaack." I looked over. Ketchup Lady was there.

"Oh no."

"My section's light, I can take her."

"No, I'm good, if you don't mind seating her."

"That woman seats herself, but I'll take her a menu." Jamie walked out to the woman, while I walked back and grabbed a pitcher of water. I passed Jamie on the way to the dining room. "She sat herself at sixteen. Her usual."

She was seated just a few tables from Dylan and William. Honestly, I was kind of glad William was there. It would give us something to laugh about later.

"Thanks, doll. Did you check the status of the ketchup at her table?"

"Yes, the bottle is half-full."

"No, it's half-*empty*," I said. I grabbed a full bottle of ketchup and, still carrying the pitcher, walked over to her. When I got to her table, Ketchup Lady looked more agitated than usual.

I set the water and ketchup down, then said, "What can I get for you?"

"I can't sit here."

You seated yourself, I thought. "Is there a problem?"

"I would say so. Why is that nigger boy in here?"

My chest froze. I glanced over at Dylan, who was showing William how to use the Spirograph. "That boy is my son," I said, my face hot. "Don't you ever call him that again!"

The woman didn't flinch. "Well, I don't like him here."

I was so angry I was shaking. "You get out of here right now before I shove this bottle of ketchup down your throat."

She looked at me in complete shock. "How dare you!"

"How dare *you*!" I shouted back.

She began looking around the diner for support. I hadn't noticed but Loretta was standing near the cash register within earshot of the altercation. "Did you hear that?" Ketchup Lady shouted to her. "Did you hear what this insolent *waitress* just said to me?"

Loretta walked over, glaring at the woman. "I heard what you said. You get out of my diner right now. And if I ever see you here again, I'll throw you out."

The woman's face was almost as red as the ketchup. "I . . . I . . ." She glanced over at Andy. "This woman just threatened me. Do your duty. This is our country!"

Suddenly I realized that William was standing next to me. He looked fierce. "This boy's father died protecting *your* country," he said slowly but forcefully. "Do you know how many black brothers of mine died so you could fatten your face? Now get out of here before I drag you outside and throw you into the gutter where you belong."

Ketchup Lady looked utterly terrified. She turned to Andy, who was watching the exchange. "He threatened my life, Officer. Arrest him."

Andy stood and walked over. "No, all I heard was you threatening him. Get out now or I'll arrest you for causing a public disturbance."

The woman was trembling now. She looked back at Dylan. I sensed she was about to say something to him when William said, "You say one word to that child and you'll regret it for the rest of your life."

"How dare you threaten me! I have connections. You're going to see the inside of a jail, mister."

William almost looked amused. "You think that scares me? You have no idea what I've seen and what I'm capable of."

The woman looked faint. Loretta stepped forward and grabbed her by the arm. "Get out of here."

Ketchup Lady stood. She looked a little wobbly, then she stumbled toward the door. Jamie walked over to the table, grabbed the bottle of ketchup, and went to the door and threw it in the direction the woman had walked off in. I heard the bottle shatter.

"Take that, you gross slob," she shouted.

I broke down crying.

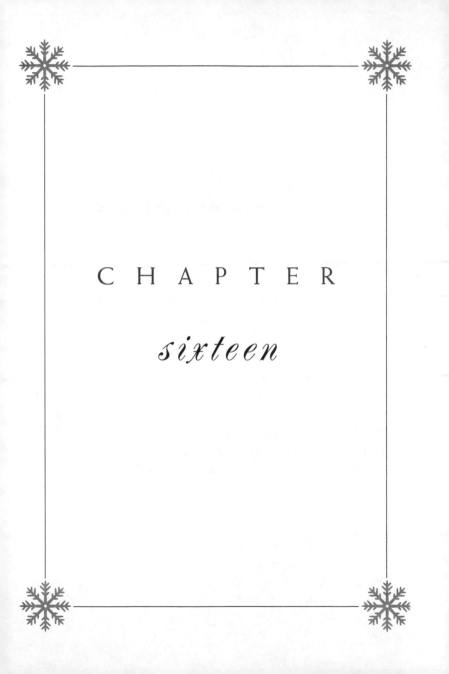

CHAPTER

sixteen

There's a reason movies use ketchup to simulate blood.
                                    —Elle Sheen's Diary

L oretta put her arm around me. "Come to the back,
honey. Come back and sit."
     "I can't," I said. "I've got to talk to Dylan." I
looked over at him. He was visibly upset.

"Did he hear what she said?" I asked William.

He shook his head. "I don't think so."

Dylan ran over to me. "Why are you crying, Mama?"

I knelt down and hugged him. William squatted down
next to us. "Everything's okay," he said. "There was a mean
lady, but we made her leave." William turned to me. "Elle,
go back with Loretta, I'll take care of Dylan." Then he said
to Dylan, "Would you like to share a milkshake?"

"No, I want my own."

"Even better," he said. "What flavor should we get?"

"Let's get strawberry."

"Perfect. I love strawberry."

Loretta smiled at him. "I'll get two strawberries. And
thank you, sir, for your service."

"You're welcome."

She turned to me. "Your friend has things under control. Now come on back, darlin'."

As we walked back she said to Andy, "Your dinner's on me, Officer. Dessert too."

"Always my pleasure," he said. "We don't need that kind of crazy in Mistletoe."

CHAPTER

seventeen

William said something tonight I won't forget: "Never live someone else's crazy."

—Elle Sheen's Diary

Loretta let me go home early. Actually, she made me. William stayed with Dylan the whole time I was in the back with Loretta. They were arm wrestling when I came out, William pretending to lose.

I was wearing my coat and carrying Dylan's over my arm. "It's time to go, Dylan."

"Okay." He started stuffing all his toys back in his bag.

William sidled up to me. He asked softly, "Are you okay?"

I just nodded. I was afraid that if I opened my mouth I'd start crying.

"May I give you a hug?"

"Yes. Please."

He put his arms around me. For a moment he just quietly held me. I almost forgot we were in public. He felt so good—his warmth, his strength.

"Can I drive you home?" he asked.

"I have my car."

"We can pick it up tomorrow after we go tubing. If you're still up for it."

"I don't know."

"We should go," he said. "We can't let crazy people dictate our lives."

He squeezed me one last time, then released me and turned back to Dylan. "Hey, tough guy. Want to go home in my truck?"

"Yay!" he said.

I took Dylan's hand and we walked out the diner's front door. I noticed something different in William's moves. He seemed aware of the movement around him; every car and every human. He was still a soldier. When he pulled up to my house he was just as vigilant, walking me to the door. I felt sorry for anyone who might think to cross him.

I opened the door. "Go inside, Dylan," I said.

He looked at William. "Can we play Rock 'Em Sock 'Em Robots?"

"It's too late tonight. But Mr. William is coming over tomorrow."

"I'll be over tomorrow morning," William said. "To take you tubing. I'll bring more chocolate."

"Yes!"

"But only if you go right to bed."

"Okay."

"And brush your teeth."

"All right."

He ran inside. I looked up at William. Before I could thank him he said, "Are you okay?"

"I'm still a little shaken up."

"There will always be people like that. Don't give them your time or your sanity."

I looked into his eyes. "Thank you for being there."

"You're safe now," he said. "You can trust me."

I looked at him for a moment, then said, "I do. I don't know why, I barely know you, but I do." I leaned my head forward against his chest.

He put his arms around me and kissed my forehead, then leaned back. "You are an amazing, beautiful woman. No wonder . . ." He stopped.

I looked up at him. "No wonder what?"

He paused. "No wonder everyone loves you."

I looked at him, not believing that that was what he had been going to say. I took a deep breath and stepped back. "I'll see you tomorrow."

"Tomorrow," he said. "Lock your door."

"I will." Up until that day I never had.

CHAPTER

eighteen

In the middle of a snowstorm we tubed down a steep hill,
blind and out of control. That pretty much describes my
life these days.

—Elle Sheen's Diary

I woke the next morning feeling refreshed and excited for the day. William arrived at my place at five minutes to nine. He wore army boots, wool gloves, and his green army jacket. I figured it was the only coat he had.

Dylan answered the door. "Hi, Mr. William. Did you bring the chocolate?"

"Dylan," I said, walking up behind him. "You don't just ask people for chocolate."

"No, he's just keeping me honest," William said. "I promised him." He brought a chocolate bar out of his jacket. "Did you go to bed?"

"Yes, sir."

"Did you brush your teeth?"

"Yes, sir."

He held out the chocolate bar. "Then you've earned this amazing bar of chocolate."

"Smart man," I replied. "Earning points with the kid."

Dylan took the candy and turned to me. "Can I?"

"Chocolate for breakfast?" I said. "Sure, why not?"

He quickly tore open the wrapper.

"Dylan, where are your gloves and hat?"

"I don't know."

"They're in your closet."

"If you knew, why did you ask?" Dylan said.

I breathed out. "Just get them."

William laughed. "He got you."

As Dylan went to his room I said to William, "Thank you again for last night."

"I would say it was a pleasure, but it wasn't."

"You're a strong man."

"When I'm not under trucks," he said.

When Dylan returned, the bar of chocolate was gone and the corners of his mouth were stained with chocolate. We walked out to William's truck and climbed into it. The bed was filled with two large inner tubes, both dusted with snow.

"Where are we going?" he asked.

"There's a little park just before the canyon," I said. "It's not far from here. The hills are just the right size for Dylan."

"Just point the way."

Twenty minutes later we arrived at the park. There were maybe a dozen others, riding tubes and sleighs.

It was snowing fairly hard and even though I had told Dylan that we wouldn't go in the snow, it was only because I was afraid to drive in it. William had no such problem.

We picked a medium-sized hill and William carried the two inner tubes up the incline while I walked up behind him holding Dylan's hand.

At the hill's summit we linked ourselves together with our legs and slid down together, screaming and laughing. At least I screamed. Dylan just laughed. I hadn't seen him that happy for some time. The falling snow limited our visibility, which added both to my fear and our general excitement. We tubed for about two hours, until we looked like animated snowmen; our clothes soaked through and almost frozen, we drove back to my house.

"That was so cool!" Dylan exclaimed, still excited from the day.

"That was a good place to tube," William said.

"It's not too steep or too crowded," I said. "Especially in the snow." I looked at him. "The county lets you cut Christmas trees there," I said. "Jamie and I cut one once. It was only a little one but we still had trouble carrying it out."

"I could help with that," he said. "If you decide to do it again."

"I might take you up on that." I leaned over and whispered, "A tree is not in the budget this year."

William whispered back, "Does Dylan know?"

I glanced over at him and then shook my head. "Not yet. I'm still hoping something might work out."

He nodded. A moment later he said, "Do we have time to stop for a hamburger?"

"I just need to be at work by three."

"Plenty of time."

William drove us to the Arctic Circle, a small local hamburger joint just a mile from Mistletoe up I-15. As we walked into the restaurant Dylan froze. There was a young black man standing behind the counter. Seeing black men in Mistletoe was rare enough, but a black teenager was a first for him.

For a moment the two of them stared at each other. William approached the counter. "How's it going?"

The young man looked away from Dylan. "Not bad. What can I get for you?"

"I'd like two Ranch burgers and an order of fries with your famous fry sauce." He turned to me. "What would you like?"

"I'll have half of what you're getting. Dylan will have the corn dog."

Dylan still just stood there staring at the young man. William turned to him. "Do you want fries with that?"

Dylan nodded.

"Got to have the fries," William said. "We'll also have two Cokes and a lime rickey. That will do it." He took his wallet from his back pocket. "Thank you."

"No problem," the young man said.

As we sat at the table Dylan suddenly said, "He's a Negro."

William nodded. "There are black people everywhere. In the army my best friends were black. This is just kind of a different town. There aren't many black people."

"How come?"

"Good question." William turned to me. "How come?"

"More are in the big cities than in small towns like ours," I said.

"Why?" Dylan asked.

"I'll have to think about that."

"Let us know when you figure that out," William said, grinning.

"So how's the corn dog?" William asked.

"Good," Dylan said.

"You know, where I used to live, sometimes they fed us fish heads."

I was surprised that he was talking about it.

Dylan stared at him, not sure if he was kidding or not. "Honest?"

"I'm telling God's truth. I wish I wasn't."

"Did you eat them?"

"You'll eat anything if you're hungry enough." He leaned forward. "Even rats."

"Ooh," Dylan said.

William nodded. "Tastes like chicken."

❄

On the way back to town William said, "We still need to pick up your car."

I had forgotten that we had left it at the diner. "I'm glad one of us remembered."

A few moments later William stopped his truck behind

the diner next to the Fairlane, which was covered with snow. "What time do you need to be back here?"

"Not until three," I said. "I have ninety minutes. Would you like to come over for some hot cocoa?"

"I would love to."

"Can Mr. William play Rock 'Em Sock 'Em Robots?" Dylan asked.

"I'm sure Mr. William has better things to do."

"Better than playing Rock 'Em Sock 'Em Robots?" he replied. "I think not." He turned to Dylan. "Are you good?"

"Yeah."

"We'll see," he said.

He turned to me, "Give me your car keys."

"How come?"

"So I can warm up your car while I clear off the snow."

I took my keys out. "You don't need to . . ."

He put his finger on my lips, stopping me. "Let me be good to you."

It was the sweetest thing I had heard in months.

He got out, pried my car door open—which had frozen shut—started my car, then, with a broom he took from the bed of his truck, cleared the snow off my windshield. Five minutes later he opened my door and offered me his hand. "It's ready. Your car's warm."

"Thank you," I said, taking it. I stepped in. "Meet you at my duplex?"

"I'll see you there."

"Can I ride with Mr. William?" Dylan asked.

"It's fine with me," William said.

"Sure."

Back at my duplex we kicked off our boots and then went inside. Dylan took William's hand and led him into his room while I went to the kitchen and heated up some milk in a saucepan, then poured in the cocoa powder. When it was hot, I poured three coffee cups full and dropped in marshmallows. I carried all three cups into Dylan's bedroom, something waitresses are good at. I gave them their drinks, then sat down on the floor next to William to watch them box.

"You're really good at this," William said to Dylan.

"You're not so good," Dylan said.

"Dylan," I said.

"He's right," William said. "I stink at this. He keeps knocking my block off."

They played a little longer until I made Dylan get in the bathtub. While he was bathing, William and I sat at the kitchen table with our cocoa. "I like your place," he said.

"Thank you. You have a nice place too."

He looked at me quizzically. "I thought you had been there."

I laughed. "I have."

"So you're either being cloyingly polite or have trouble seeing in the dark."

I smiled. "It was a little dark. And I'm a little cloying."

William laughed.

"Who lives in the other side of the duplex?"

"Mr. Foster."

"What's he like?"

"Old, mostly. He rarely comes out."

"But he's quiet?"

"Not really. I mean, he is; it's not like he's having wild parties, but his hearing's going, so he turns the TV all the way up. Fortunately, he goes to bed before Dylan does."

"Is he nice?"

"Yes, and he pays Dylan a dollar to take his garbage to the curb. That's like a nickel a foot."

"What does Dylan do with all that money?"

"I make him put it in his college fund."

We drank our cocoa.

"Today was a nice day," I said.

"Yeah, it was. Dylan's a great kid."

"He's my reason, you know? He's proof of God's love."

"He's proof of your love," William said.

"I worry about him. Like, maybe I'm going to ruin his life by living here."

"Why do you think that?"

"He's the only black child in his school. He's the only black child in this whole town. You saw how he reacted to that young man at the hamburger place. Then add to that the fact that he doesn't have a father."

"He has you. And father or not, you've done a great job with him."

"I just wish I could give him a better life."

"You give him love. That's better than anything material you could give him."

"I know. I just wish I could give him more time. I work so much." I shook my head. "I keep waiting for things to get easier, but they don't."

"Who watches Dylan when you're working?"

"Fran."

"She's the one I met the other night?"

"Yes. She's like a second mother to him."

"How did you find her?"

"She worked at the diner for a while, but she didn't last long. She's in college now."

"Speaking of the diner . . ." He glanced down at his watch. "It's almost time for you to go to work. I better go."

Just then Dylan came out of the bathroom wearing only Flash Gordon underwear. "Want to play Rock 'Em Sock 'Em again?"

"Hmm," William said. "Let's see, do I want to be beaten and humiliated again? I don't think so."

"Please?"

"As fun as it sounds, I think I'd better go home. Your mom needs to go to work, and your sitter will be here soon."

Dylan turned to me. "Can Mr. William watch me?"

"No, honey. Fran is coming."

Dylan looked disappointed.

"I'll be back," William said. He looked at me. "If it's okay with your mother."

Dylan looked up at me. "Is it, Mama?"

"Absolutely," I said. "Now say goodbye to Mr. William, then I'm going to step outside to talk to him."

"Goodbye, Mr. William."

"Goodbye, Dylan."

I led William outside, shutting the door behind me. "That's quite an honor. He wants you to watch him instead of Fran."

"Probably because he can beat me at the boxing robots."

"Probably," I said with a half smile. "Thank you for taking us tubing. And to lunch. Dylan had a really good time."

"Do you think Dylan's mother had a good time too?"

I smiled. "She had a good time too."

"Good," he said. "I was kind of going for that."

"So, before you go, I wanted to ask you something." As he looked at me I suddenly felt a little nervous.

"Yes?"

"I wanted to ask what are you doing for Thanksgiving?"

"Thanksgiving. What Thanksgiving?"

"So you don't have plans."

"No, I have plans. I've got a date with myself and a turkey-and-mashed-potatoes TV dinner. Hold the TV."

"I'd hate to interrupt that feast, but would you like to have dinner with Dylan and me? I can pretty much guarantee that the food will be better."

"Not to mention the company," he said. "I absolutely bore myself. Sometimes I get in arguments with myself just to stir things up."

I smiled.

"What can I bring?"

"Just your boring, argumentative self," I said. "I get almost everything from the diner."

"Then how about I bring some wine?" he said.

"I won't turn you down on that."

"I didn't think so. So do I have to wait until Thanksgiving to see you again?"

I smiled. "I'm off Tuesday at three."

"Can you find a sitter?"

"I'll get a sitter."

"I promise I'll make it worth your while."

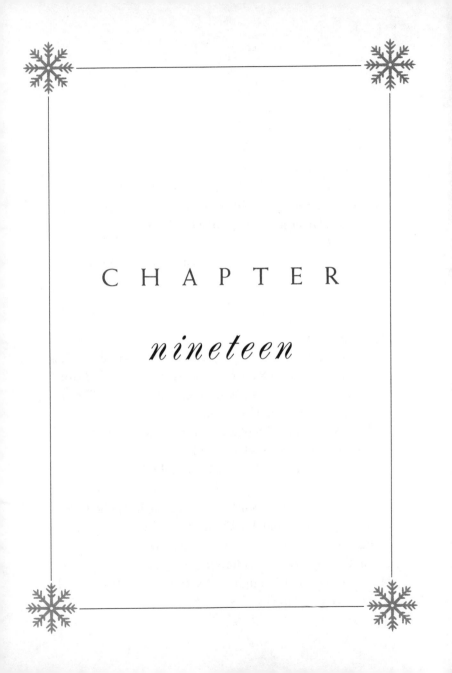

CHAPTER

nineteen

We do not always believe things because they're true. More often than not, we believe things because they're expedient.

—Elle Sheen's Diary

MONDAY, NOVEMBER 24

Monday night after work, Fran met me outside the duplex, which is something she never did unless she was in a hurry to get somewhere. She stood in front of the door as if she were guarding it. "You'll never believe what happened," she said.

"I'm sure I won't," I replied. "Is it a good or bad thing?"

"Two things. First, Dylan is still up."

Bad thing, I thought. "It's a school night."

"I know, but I made a judgment call. I think you would have done the same. Something special happened." She opened the door and I walked in. In the middle of our living room was a six-foot Christmas tree. It was mostly decorated and Dylan was standing next to it laying strands of tinsel across its boughs. His smile was epic. "Look, Mama! We got a tree!"

I turned to Fran. "Where did it come from?"

"Well, we all went on an unexpected little field trip."

"A field trip?"

"Literally. William came by in his truck and we went to a field and cut it down. He set it up, and Dylan and I did the decorations."

I glanced around. "Where's William?"

"He left a couple hours ago. He said 'Merry Christmas' and he'll see you tomorrow." She shook her head. "It's kind of a Christmas miracle."

"He's kind of a Christmas miracle," I replied.

❋

I found I was thinking about him all the time. I couldn't wait until Tuesday. How different my life felt having something to look forward to.

William wouldn't tell me what we were doing as he wanted it to be a surprise. His only instruction to me was to dress for winter and wear warm boots. So I threw on a turtleneck sweater and jeans and wondered if we were going hiking again. We didn't. He picked me up a little after four o'clock and we drove north up I-15.

We were going for a sleigh ride. It was dusk when we arrived at Hardware Ranch about an hour north of Mistletoe near Hyrum. The ranch was state-owned and encompassed nearly twenty thousand acres.

Dylan would have loved it, but I'm glad we went alone. William and I snuggled up together under a blanket for the hour-long ride, which took us through miles of pristine wilderness and past the largest herd of elk I'd ever seen. Our driver told us that the herd had started with a couple dozen and then grew over the past decade to nearly a thousand animals.

After the ride we drove to the nearby town of Brigham City (named after the Mormon prophet Brigham Young) and had dinner at a little restaurant called the Maddox Ranch House. The restaurant was one of the oldest in Utah and had garnered a reputation of having some of the state's best fried chicken, bison steaks, and hot buttered rolls.

We both ordered comfort food. William ordered the breaded trout while I had the chicken-fried steak with mashed potatoes.

"Thank you for the tree," I said again. "You should have seen how excited Dylan was."

"I did," he said.

"Of course. Was it hard getting the tree out?"

"A little. I could have used a horse to help pull it out," he said, buttering a roll. "Speaking of which, you seemed comfortable around the horses tonight."

"I grew up with horses," I said. "My father raises them. At least he did. I have no idea if he still does."

"So your dad was a horse breeder."

"My dad was into a lot of things. He was in the military until he was thirty-five, then he retired and bought the ranch in Cedar City. He's an entrepreneur and an investor. We never wanted for anything.

"Growing up, we lived frugally—my father wore old clothes, mowed his own lawn, drove an old car—but I realize now we were well off. My dad wasn't showy, and he's not obsessed with money; it just kind of flows with him." I looked at William. "Does that make sense?"

He nodded. "I knew people like that in the military."

"I certainly didn't inherit it from him. I've been poor since the minute I left home."

He grinned. "You mean you're not getting rich at the diner?"

"No. Are you getting rich at Renato's?"

"What do you think?"

"I hear Renato is as tight as a tourniquet."

"That's a little harsh. Renato has been good to me," William said. "I'm not getting rich, but I don't really need much either. When I got back from the war, I had a lot of back pay from the military, so I've got savings. I'm doing okay."

"This is an odd question, but do you get paid as a POW?"

"It's considered time served. POWs also get a little extra—sixty-five dollars a month, for imminent danger pay. Sounds absurd hearing it that way: I made an extra two dollars a day for putting my life in greater danger."

He took a bite of his fish, then said, "You also progress through the ranks, so your salary goes up." He smiled darkly. "I didn't get to do a whole lot of shopping in Hanoi, so the money just stacked up."

"You said you were sent to Vietnam by a judge."

He nodded. "I was facing hard jail time."

"That's hard for me to believe."

"Why is that?"

"Because you're one of the sweetest men I've ever met."

He smiled at the comment. "I put on a good show."

"I don't think so. I'm a pretty good judge of character," I said. "What's your family like?"

"Dead."

His reply stunned me. He noticed.

"Sorry," he said quickly. "That was . . . crass."

"That's okay," I said.

"The truth is, I had a great family and an idyllic childhood. I had both parents at home, two little sisters, Little League baseball on Saturday, church on Sundays. We were pretty much the Cleaver family—until they were killed in a car crash."

"Your whole family?"

He nodded. "Everyone but me. I was supposed to be with them, but I got in a fight with my mother before leaving and said I wouldn't go. I was stubborn. I locked myself in my room. My dad wouldn't have put up with that nonsense. He would have knocked my door down and dragged me out, but he wasn't there. He was in Ohio on business. He was an auto parts salesman. My mother and sisters met up with him and were headed to Cincinnati for the week."

"What was the fight about?"

William shook his head. "I don't remember. I should have been with them."

"You would have died if you were."

"I'm not sure that would have been such a bad thing."

The comment hurt my heart. "Maybe you weren't supposed to be with them. Maybe God was looking out for you."

"I'm not that fatalistic," he said. "It would make me wonder why He wasn't looking after them." After a while he breathed out. "After they died, I had no one. We had one of those isolated families where neither of my parents had any familial connections. My father didn't get along with his family, and my mother didn't have one. I think she was an accident. She was an only child and born late in her parents' lives. Her father was sixty-five when she was born. Her mother was fifty-two. Her father died when she was nine, her mother passed away the same year I was born.

"So with no family and since I wasn't yet eighteen, I became a ward of the state and was put in the foster care system. It didn't go well. At that age, I was too old to assimilate into another family. Not to mention, I was pretty messed up. My family had just died and the last thing I had said to my mother was that I hated her. The guilt and shame were eating me alive. I think some part of me blamed myself for their deaths."

"You know that's not true."

"I know—I knew it then—but I didn't *believe* it. Belief and knowledge aren't the same thing. Belief is much more powerful.

"During that time I actually tried to join the army, but I was too young. So I ended up as a foster child with a caseworker. I honor anyone who takes in a foster child, but the family I was put with was a mistake. They owned a dry-cleaning business and were basically looking for free labor. I was working sixty hours a week cleaning and pressing clothes. I told my caseworker that I was a slave, but she just thought I was exaggerating. Finally, after a year and a half of that, I ran away.

"I couch-hopped for a while, then I got a job with one of my dad's old clients at a car dealership detailing cars. It was a pretty good gig. Then one day, at the dealership, I ran into a group of guys a few years older than me. I thought they were cool. They talked tough, and they had hot cars and foxy girlfriends. They all shared an old home together, kind of like a commune. None of them worked; they just, like, hung out all day. One of them invited me to move into their place. They gave me cigarettes and beer. I thought I was pretty cool because they liked me.

"It never occurred to me how they were supporting their lifestyle. I didn't realize they made their money stealing or that they brought me in because they were grooming me for something. One night after a few months, they came to me and said, 'You've been living off us far too long. It's time you earned your keep.' I had no idea what they were talking about, but they told me that if I didn't help them break into the car dealership I worked at, they were going to beat me up for freeloading and then make me pay them back for all the food and beer and back rent.

"I offered them all the money I had, but they came up with some ridiculous amount of money I owed them, like five thousand dollars, nothing I could have afforded.

"So I helped them break in. They stole two cars. Then one of the security men walked in on us. One of the guys had a gun and shot him. It didn't kill him, thankfully, but it was considered attempted murder.

"The security guard recognized me and we were caught. I had just turned eighteen a week before, so I was tried as an adult. Those guys I thought were so cool showed their real colors; they told the court it was all my idea. Since I worked at the dealership, the judge believed them. It was their word against mine.

"That's when he gave me the option to go to Vietnam or prison. I had already tried to join the army, so it was pretty much a no-brainer for me."

"And I thought I had it tough," I said.

"What I went through doesn't make your life any easier," he said. Then he forced a smile, saying, "That conversation turned heavy fast. Let's talk about something lighter."

I smiled back. "Like what?"

"Like, did you know your name is a palindrome?"

"What's a palindrome?"

"It's something that reads the same forward and backward. Like the words *radar* or *racecar.*"

I worked it out in my head. "*Racecar.* That's kind of cool."

"They can be more than one word," he said. "My favorite palindromes are *Do geese see God?* and the world's first greeting, 'Madam, I'm Adam.'"

"You know, the man they named Noel Street for was a palindrome. His name was Leon Noel."

"I assumed they named it Noel Street because the town's name is kind of . . . Christmassy." He looked at me. "Is that a word?"

"Christmassy. Works for me," I said. "Mistletoe is definitely Christmassy. You arrived just in time for the Noel Street Christmas Market."

"I saw them putting up booths in the park," he said. Suddenly his expression softened. "Fort Wayne used to have something like that. They called it 'Christmas in the Park.' It was only one day, but there'd be horse-drawn wagon rides and groups singing carols. They had booths with crafts and things. There were food vendors, hot wassail, eggnog, and fresh donuts." His eyes had the soft glaze of nostalgia. "We used to go there every year as a family . . ."

"Dylan and I look forward to the market every year. This year will be the best ever."

"Why is that?"

I looked at him and smiled. "Because you're here."

❄

William dropped me off at home a little before midnight. He walked me to the door. "So I'll see you on Thursday?"

"What's Thursday?" he asked.

I glared at him.

He grinned. "Oh, right. Thanksgiving."

"Oh, Thanksgiving," I mocked.

"I'll come hungry," he said.

"I promise you won't leave that way."

"I believe you." He looked into my eyes. The mood grew more serious. "I had a really good time tonight."

"Me too."

Then he leaned forward and we kissed for the first time. It was delicious.

After we separated I said, "Thank you again for tonight."

"I'll see you Thursday."

He turned and walked back to his truck. I waved as he drove off, then went inside. Fran was at the kitchen table doing homework. She looked up at me wearily. "How was the date?"

I smiled. "Perfect."

"Perfect," she repeated. "I think that's good."

My brow fell. "Why do you say that?"

"I don't know. It's just, where do you go from perfect?"

CHAPTER

twenty

For better or worse, this is a Thanksgiving I will never forget.
                                                    —Elle Sheen's Diary

Thanksgiving was special. For starters, I got the day off with pay. The diner was closed. It's not that there wasn't enough business. The opposite was true. Thanksgiving always provided a stream of travelers, truck drivers, and Eleanor Rigbys but, as a courtesy to her staff, Loretta shut the place down.

What made the day even better was a self-imposed tradition started by our chef Bart. The day before Thanksgiving Bart made a meal for all of our families, which included his delectable cornbread stuffing, pecan-crusted sweet-potato soufflé, Parker House rolls (just the dough so we could serve them hot), and mashed potatoes with turkey gravy. For dessert I purchased one of Loretta's famous Granny Smith apple pies, the kind with a cinnamon-and-sugar latticework crust. Instant Thanksgiving, just add turkey.

Or, in our case, roast chicken. Dylan liked chicken more than turkey, and since it was the right size for the two of us, that's what we usually had. But this year with William coming, I opted for the larger species of bird.

❄

What I will always remember about that Thanksgiving is that the day started out good, ended good, and the dash between the two ends was a nightmare.

It was snowing again when William arrived at noon. I had just brought out the turkey and the rolls were almost brown, so I asked him to carve the turkey, something he was keen to do, while I brought out the piping-hot rolls and saw to the rest of the meal. We set all the food out on the kitchen counter, then sat together around our tiny kitchen table.

"I'll pray," I said. "Let's hold hands." I cleared my throat. "God, we thank Thee for the remarkable abundance of our lives. We are grateful that William has chosen to spend this day with us. Please bless us to serve all Thy children, especially those that are without. Amen."

"Amen," my men echoed.

I wondered if William had had a decent Thanksgiving since his childhood. He ate three plates of food, and two helpings of pie.

"Remarkable," William said, "I don't think I've ever been this full. I might pop."

Dylan looked concerned. "Really?"

"No. But you should probably wear a raincoat just in case."

Dylan looked at me. "He's kidding," I said.

"Only about the popping part," he said. His face suddenly took on a softer expression. "How life can change.

There was a time I was so hungry that I chewed on my shoe just to taste something."

"Yuck," Dylan said.

I looked at William sympathetically and took his hand.

"Why didn't you just go to the refrigerator?" Dylan asked.

He looked at Dylan, then suddenly smiled. "I should have thought of that."

After dinner Dylan went to his room to play while I made William and myself some coffee.

"Cream and sugar?" I asked.

"Both, please."

I brought the cups over.

"This is good," he said. "What is it?"

"It's a special Kona coffee bean that Loretta buys. We don't serve it; it's too expensive for our customers' tastes. But she gives it to us at cost."

"Membership at the diner has its privileges. Including this amazing dinner."

I looked at him happily. "What you said earlier, about chewing your shoe. Was that true?"

"Yes."

"How did you keep going?"

"Some say it's the survival instinct. But I don't think so."

"Why is that?"

"Nearly a million people take their lives each year. It's not about survival; it's about finding meaning in living. Even in our suffering."

"And you found meaning?"

"In a twisted way, I didn't want to let them win." He shook his head. "Whatever it takes, I guess."

"It got you here," I said.

Just then there was a loud crash in the front room. William and I entered the living room. There was a grapefruit-sized stone in the middle of the floor. Dylan came out of his room to see what the noise was. William said to Dylan, "Stay here." William ran to the window and looked out, but whoever had thrown it was gone.

We both walked over to the stone. Written on it in Magic Marker was one word: NIGGER.

William pushed the stone under the couch with his foot. "We're getting out of here," he said.

I think I was in shock. "Where?"

"My place." He said in a voice surprisingly calm, "Dylan, how would you like to play at my house?"

"Can I?" he asked.

"We'll all go," I said.

❄

Where I was paralyzed with fear, William seemed to be activated by it. "Do you want to pack some things?"

I went into Dylan's room and came out with his backpack. We drove in William's truck to the side of his building, walking through thick snow to the lobby. The brindled cat I'd seen the first day was sitting on the balustrade looking down on us.

"You have a cat?" Dylan asked.

"He's not mine," William said. "He doesn't belong to anyone. He just lives here. He might be the landlord."

"What's his name?"

"I've named him Ho Chi Minh. Because he likes to sneak up on you when you're not looking."

We walked up the stairs to William's apartment and went inside. I took Dylan's coat off and then my own. I noticed William left his on.

"Can I have the keys to your house?" he asked.

"Yes." I took them out of my purse and handed them to him. "How come?"

"I'm going to get some cardboard and patch up your window so the snow doesn't come in. I'll be back in an hour. Don't let anyone in."

"Do you think we're in danger?"

"No. But I don't take chances."

He walked out. "Where is Mr. William going?" Dylan asked.

"He just went to fix something," I said.

"How come someone threw a rock through our window?"

I didn't know that he had comprehended what had happened.

"I don't know. Sometimes people do strange things because they're afraid."

Dylan looked more puzzled. "What are they afraid of?"

"Things they don't understand," I said. "What scares you?"

"Bears," he said.

I nodded. "Me too."

"Did a bear throw that rock?"

"Maybe," I said. "Maybe."

❄

While William was gone I cleaned his apartment: washed the dishes, dusted, even mopped the floor with a cloth. The air was a little stale, so I turned up the heat and cracked a window to let some fresh air in. An hour and a half later William returned. He looked around his apartment.

"You cleaned."

"I had to keep busy," I said. "How did it go?"

"I boarded up the window. I cleaned up the glass and then took the stone over to the police station. That one officer was there."

"Andy?"

"No, the short one with a crew cut."

"Peter," I said. "What did he say?"

"He asked if we saw anything. I told him we didn't, so he's going to check with your neighbors to see if they saw anything." He looked at me intensely. "He asked if you had any enemies they should know about."

The question angered me. I didn't have time to make enemies. I just lived my life the best I could.

"Not that I know of," I said.

"I told him about the Ketchup Lady."

"What did he say?"

"The other officer had already told him about what happened at the diner. He's driving over to her house later today to interrogate her."

"He knows who she is?"

"Loretta did. She looked her up once—just in case she ended up causing any problems."

My heart hurt. I looked over at Dylan, who was still in the bedroom. "So what do we do now?"

"I say we go for a ride and not let this nastiness ruin our holiday."

"Where?"

"How about Salt Lake?" he said. "I heard that they turn the lights on at Temple Square Thanksgiving night."

"Whatever you think," I said. The truth was, I was tired of always being in charge and having to figure out what to do. For once I just wanted to be looked out for. "When?"

"Now."

I walked back to the bedroom. "Come on, Dylan. We're going for a ride."

CHAPTER

twenty-one

My heart feels like a kite in a hurricane.
                                    —Elle Sheen's Diary

The drive to Salt Lake was slow. I-15 was slick and we found ourselves following a caravan of snowplows. I didn't care. We weren't in any hurry.

When we arrived at the downtown area we were surprised at how empty the square was. William stopped at the curb near the center and got out. He asked someone wearing a name tag what time they turned the lights on. He walked back to me. "Well, I messed that up. They turn them on the day after Thanksgiving."

"It's okay," I said. "It's still pretty. Let's walk around the grounds."

The truth was, I wasn't disappointed. In my state of mind I wasn't really in the mood to fight crowds. It just felt good to be somewhere else. Mostly, it felt good to be with William.

We walked around the Temple grounds and then through one of the nearby indoor malls called the ZCMI Center. Our Thanksgiving gluttony had started to wear off, which we satiated with Chinese noodles, caramel apples, and saltwater taffy.

The evening was calm and pleasant and, by dusk, I'd almost forgotten why we'd left Mistletoe to begin with. On the way back home Dylan fell asleep on my lap.

"Looks like we wore him out," William said, glancing over.

"It's usually the other way around," I said.

"Sorry I mixed up the night."

"I wouldn't change a thing," I said.

"You can lean against me, if you want."

I lay my head against his shoulder. We didn't speak much, in part because Dylan was sleeping, but mostly because the silence was enough. We drove back to his apartment.

"I think you should stay at my place tonight," he said softly. "You and Dylan can sleep in the bed. I'll sleep on the couch."

I just nodded. William carried Dylan inside and I tucked him into the bed that I had slept next to when I was taking care of William that first night.

"I don't have anything to wear," I said. In my hurry to leave I'd only packed for Dylan.

"I might have something," William said. He opened a drawer and pulled out a T-shirt with the Harley-Davidson logo on it. "Try this. It might be long enough."

He stepped out of the room. I took off everything except my underwear and donned the long T-shirt. It fell to my knees. I opened the door. "It fits."

He looked at me. "You look cute."

"If the shirt fits . . ."

For a moment he just looked at me. Maybe longingly. Or maybe I just hoped.

"Is there anything else I can get for you?" he asked.

I walked over and hugged him. "Thank you for being so sweet. Today should have been awful. But I feel happy."

"So do I," he said. "Thank you for inviting me to dinner."

"Thank you for coming."

As I looked into his eyes I felt drawn to him. Into him. We began kissing. It was several minutes before I pulled away. "I better go to bed," I said reluctantly.

He just looked into my eyes. "Are you sure?"

I nodded. "Yeah. Good night."

"Good night," he said. He kissed me once more, then sat down on the couch. "Sleep well."

"You too," I said.

I went back inside the bedroom and shut the door behind me.

I couldn't sleep. I could still taste his lips on mine. For more than an hour I just lay in the dark thinking about him. Wanting him. I looked over at Dylan to make sure he was asleep, then I pulled the covers up to his chin and got out of bed. I walked to the door, opened it, stepped out, and quietly pulled it shut behind me. William was asleep on the couch. He was mumbling a little.

I knelt down on the floor next to him, then put my hand on his side. He stopped talking. Then he slowly turned around, his eyes open. "I want to lay with you," I whispered.

He just looked at me, his eyes gently studying my face, then moved as far back against the couch as he could and rolled onto his side, giving me a small perch to rest my body next to his. I climbed onto the couch, our faces just inches apart from each other. The darkness caressed his shadowed face. For a long time we just gazed into each other's eyes. Then I said, "I'm falling for you."

He just looked back at me with soft eyes. "Don't. I'm broken."

"I know."

His eyes suddenly welled with tears, which pooled above his nose and fell down his face. I gently touched the tears with my fingers and wiped them off. Then I pressed my lips to his and we kissed, softly, sweetly at first, then passionately. Everything around us dissolved into nothing. Only once before in my life had I felt that kind of love.

CHAPTER

twenty-two

Sometimes we need the darkness to reveal our light.
—Elle Sheen's Diary

FRIDAY, NOVEMBER 28

I woke the next morning in William's bed next to Dylan. Somewhere in the night William must have carried me back to his room. I was disappointed to not feel his body next to mine, but I was glad. It would have been confusing for Dylan had he come out of the room and found us together.

With Dylan still asleep, I got dressed and went into the living room. William was gone. I didn't know what that meant.

Ten minutes later I heard the front door open. William walked in. His shoulders had snow on them and he was carrying a bag from the grocery store.

"I got us something for breakfast," he said.

I took the sack from him and set it on the counter. Then I helped him off with his jacket, which he flung to the floor, and I put my arms around him, my head against his chest. He wrapped his arms around me. I wanted to be held by him more than I could say. I didn't know how he felt about what had passed between us during the night but I knew what I felt. I said softly, "I meant what I said last night."

He kissed the top of my head. "I know."

I knew he was having trouble saying how he felt about me. Of course, I wanted to hear it, but I didn't care right then. He had already said it, just without words. He had shown me he cared in a hundred ways. He had shown me with his strength and anger and gentleness and vulnerability. I would rather have someone show me love and not tell me than tell me and not show me. I think we're all that way.

"Is Dylan still asleep?"

I smiled. "You'd know it if he wasn't," I said. "Do you have any eggs?"

"Maybe half a dozen."

"I can make French toast. Would you like that?"

"Yes."

"Sit down at the table. Let me serve you."

"I'd rather be next to you."

I smiled. "Me too."

He stood behind me with his arms around my waist. It was romantic but not very practical to cook like that. I finally turned around and we kissed. After several minutes I breathlessly said, "Maybe you should sit on the couch or we'll never eat."

He smiled, kissed me again, then walked over and sat down. As I worked I occasionally glanced over at him. His eyes were always on me, as if he were transfixed by me.

I made coffee and cocoa and French toast, then took the remaining French toast batter and cooked it up into a light scramble.

"I don't have syrup," he said.

"You have sugar," I said. "I can make that work." I dissolved brown sugar and water together, then buttered a couple of pieces of toast for Dylan and put the rest on a single plate and poured syrup over the top. Then I scooped up the egg and put it next to the toast. I brought the plate to the table. "Breakfast is served."

"Where's your plate?"

"I'll share yours."

He took a bite, then forked a bite for me. I opened my mouth and he fed me. I stared at him as I ate as if I couldn't take my eyes off him. We ate the whole meal this way.

"Do you have to work today?" he asked.

"Tonight." I looked at him. "How about you?"

"Usual day."

"Could you drop by the diner after work? I'll feed you."

"I'll stay until closing if you want."

I smiled. "That would be nice."

He sat back. "Until we find out what happened, it would probably be best if Dylan didn't go back to your place." He added, "He could stay here."

"I think it would be better if he stayed with Fran. It would be more natural."

"Whatever you think is best."

I fed him the last bite of French toast. "Could you drive me to my car?"

"Your car's already downstairs."

"How did you get it here?"

"I got Sam at the grocery store to drive it over."

"Thank you."

"You're welcome." He lifted our plate and stood. "I better get to work." He took our plate to the sink and set it in water. "Would you like me to find someone to repair your window?"

"No, I'll call the landlady. She's good about things like that."

"All right. I guess I'll go." He just looked at me as he breathed out slowly. "You make it hard to go."

I walked over to him and we kissed. "Thank you for making me feel safe."

"Thank you for letting me."

CHAPTER

twenty-three

I'm afraid I'm falling for him. That's a lie. I've hit the ground without a chute.

—Elle Sheen's Diary

Dylan and I returned to our duplex a little after noon. Not only had William picked up the broken glass from the window and put cardboard over it but he'd cleaned up after the Thanksgiving meal as well, wrapping the leftovers in plastic wrap or putting them in Tupperware. He had even vacuumed, which to me is one of the most romantic things a man can do.

Gretchen, my landlady, was her typical efficient self and had someone there to repair the window even before it was time for me to leave for work. Dylan sat in the living room watching the man replace the window and chatting the poor man's ears off.

Fran arrived around two as the window repairman was finishing up. Outside our door was the previous window's frame with its remaining shards and Fran had walked in past it, leaving her visibly upset.

"Did they catch who did it?" she asked.

"Not yet," I said.

"People are sick."

I looked at her softly. "Some are."

✳

I got Dylan off with Fran and then drove to work.

Word about the stone being thrown through our window had already spread around the diner and Loretta was eager to talk to me about it.

"I'm sure it's that vile Katherine woman," she said. "It can't be a coincidence."

"Who's Katherine?" I asked.

"Aka Ketchup Lady. You know I gave Andy her address. He and Peter went out to interrogate her."

"I don't know if it was her or not," I said. "I just don't ever want to see her again."

"You know you won't see her here. She steps one foot in here and she gets the boot. She can slurp her ketchup somewhere else."

"Thanks for the support."

"That's what I'm here for, baby girl."

William came in around seven. He sat himself in my section and got up and kissed me when I came out to him.

"Did you get your window fixed?" he asked.

"Yes. And the strangest thing, my house was clean. Sparkling, even."

"Christmas elves," he said.

"Apparently," I said. "I wonder why they came only after you moved into town."

"Coincidence, maybe."

"I think not." I grinned. "What are you doing tomorrow?"

"Working. Renato got backed up. I told him I'd work him out of his mess."

"All day?"

"All day, all night. Sorry, you know I'd rather be with you. I'm open Sunday, though. Do you have anything Sunday?"

"Church. But that's just until one." A thought crossed my mind. "Why don't you come to church with us?"

"I don't do church," he said.

"You might like it." I grabbed his hand. "I'll be there. Then I'll cook you a nice meal after."

"We could have Thanksgiving leftovers," he said.

"That sounds like a yes."

"Yes. What time?"

"Church starts at eleven, so if you're picking us up, ten thirty would be good."

"I'll be there."

"I have two more events to put on your calendar."

"I don't have a calendar," he said.

"That makes it easy, then. The first is Saturday night, December sixth. It's the Noel Street Christmas Festival. The second is Friday, December twelfth, Dylan's Christmas concert at school."

"You're planning things two weeks out?"

"Of course. You have to plan these things out," I said. "Don't you?"

"No, I just go with the wind," he said. "I'm a drifter."

"Well, would this drifter like to join us at the annual Christmas concert?"

"Absolutely. Sounds exciting."

"Don't get too excited," I said. "It's just the usual elementary-school production. One of the teachers plays the piano while the kids sing the classics, 'Frosty the Snowman,' 'Rudolph,' 'Jingle Bells.' But Dylan's pretty excited about it. This year he got chosen to be one of the bell ringers for 'Jingle Bells.'" I grinned. "It's a big honor."

"Sounds like it," he said.

"It's during the day. Can you miss an hour of work?"

"Renato doesn't care when I work, just that I get things done. I can go in a little early."

I smiled. "I'll let Dylan know. He'll be excited."

"That makes two of us," he said. "And I thought this was going to be a boring Christmas."

CHAPTER

twenty-four

William taught me more about my own religious beliefs today than a flock of pastors and a stack of Bibles ever could.

—Elle Sheen's Diary

As I wrote before, my Sunday routine rarely varied, which, outside of my time with Dylan, is probably the biggest reason why I loved the day. It was truly a day of rest. First, unless I was filling in for someone, I never worked on Sunday. Second, I slept in almost an hour later than usual—a cherished extravagance—then, while Dylan slept, I enjoyed some quiet time with some coffee and a book. Around nine, I made Dylan his traditional Sunday waffles for breakfast.

After doing the dishes, I laid out Dylan's Sunday clothes—usually jeans, a button-down shirt, and a clip-on bow tie—then got myself ready for church. The only difference this Sunday was that William was coming, so I spent more time on my makeup and hair and worried about what to wear. I wore a long V-necked sage-green dress with an accenting fabric rose made of the same material. I had bought the dress three years earlier for one of Jamie's weddings.

I hoped William would think I looked pretty. Dylan did.

"Wow, Mama. You look beautiful."

I smiled. "Thank you."

"You don't even look like yourself."

I shook my head. "Thank you."

William showed up at my apartment at ten thirty sharp. Maybe it was still the soldier in him or maybe he was just that way, but he was always punctual. He was wearing jeans and a button-down shirt beneath a navy-blue cardigan.

"Is this okay?" he asked, looking down at himself. "I wasn't sure how I was supposed to dress. I'm not really a churchgoing guy."

"You look nice."

"Thank you. Not as nice as you."

Dylan just stood there looking at William. "I don't want to wear a tie," he said.

"Nothing in the Bible about wearing ties," I said. "But you do look nice in it."

"Your mother's right," William said. "You look pretty debonair with the tie."

"What's that mean?" he asked.

"It's an old word for *handsome*," William said.

Dylan thought for a moment, then said, "I'll wear it."

The church Dylan and I had been attending was a non-denominational Christian church that met in what had been an old funeral parlor out in the countryside almost halfway between Mistletoe and the equally small town of Wilden, falling on the latter's side of the city line.

My first Sunday in Mistletoe, Loretta told me about the

church and took me but she stopped going shortly after. I continued going without her. Fran attended the church as well.

We walked into the chapel just a few minutes before the service began. The three of us sat together in the middle of a pew next to Fran, who had come early to save us seats.

The church was small and poor. Our pastor, Pastor Henderson, did yard care and blade sharpening on the side to make ends meet.

We had a pianist, Mrs. Glad, who played an old upright piano that, I was told, had come from a bar. The church had a small choral group made up mostly of elderly parish-ioners who used to be able to sing, but still joyfully (and by joyfully I mostly mean loudly) offered what they had left. As it was the Christmas season, they sang Christmas songs, two of which the congregation joined in on: "O Come, All Ye Faithful" and "Angels We Have Heard on High."

After Pastor Henderson made a few announcements, there was another song followed by prayer, and then a Communion of grape juice and a Ritz cracker—always Dylan's favorite part of the service. This was followed by a sermon.

I loved my church and I had come to love celebrating the holiday season there. The message of hope filled my heart with peace and gratitude, both powerful forces to get me through the daily challenges of my little life. The sermon that day was on forgiveness, and Pastor Hender-son was in good form.

About ten minutes into the sermon William handed me the keys to his truck and whispered in my ear, "I'll meet you at your apartment." He stood up and made his way down the pew past the other worshippers on his way out.

I turned to Fran. "Would you take Dylan home?"

"Got it," she said, watching William leave.

I stood up and walked out after him. When I got outside the church, William was already a surprisingly long way from the chapel, walking briskly through the snow-clad barren landscape toward the main road. I couldn't believe he was walking home. It was at least seven miles to Mistletoe, and he wasn't even wearing a coat.

"William!" I shouted.

He kept walking, bent against the cold.

I shouted again as I ran toward him. "William!"

He stopped and turned around. When I caught up to him I paused to catch my breath, then said, "Where are you going?"

"I just had to get out of there," he said.

"How come?"

"I don't belong."

"Everyone belongs," I said.

"I don't," he said. "All that talk about grace and forgiveness." He looked at me. "I just couldn't handle it."

"Why?"

He hesitated. "Because God will never forgive me for what I've done."

His words moved me. "That's why God came. That's what Christmas is about. Forgiveness and hope."

"There is no hope for me. Not after what I've done."

I pondered his words, then said, "Have you ever really shared what happened with anyone?"

"No."

"Maybe it's time." I took his hand. "I want you to tell me about it."

He looked at me like I'd just asked him to jump off a cliff. Maybe I had. "I can't."

"What are you afraid of?"

He raked his hand back through his hair and looked at me. "That you won't like me anymore."

I looked him in the eyes. "My husband wrote me about the war. I know he hid a lot from me, but I could still feel both the horror and shame he felt. You were put in a situation that wasn't your fault. Would you have done those things if you hadn't been taken from your home and ordered to kill?"

He shook his head. "No, of course not."

"The fact that you're suffering shows who you really are. You need to let it go. You don't need to worry about me not loving you. You can trust me."

"Not with this." He looked up. "I don't want to take that chance."

"You have to," I said softly.

"Why?"

"Because if you believe that I couldn't love you if I knew the real you, then you will never believe in my love."

He just looked at me for a moment, then slowly nodded. "Let's go someplace."

"Let's go to your place," I said.

"My apartment?"

"No, the frozen waterfall."

"That would be appropriate," he said.

We held hands as we walked back to the church and got in his truck. We drove up along the canyon to the waterfall. No one was there, but the wind was blowing hard, so we didn't get out of the truck. We just sat inside, the heater on high.

I knew this would be difficult for him so I started. "Where do you want to begin?"

He took a deep breath. "Christmas Day." He went quiet. I reached over and took his hand.

"Tell me."

He took a deep breath. "The day started with a Christmas service put on by our chaplain. It was nostalgic, you know. Everyone was melancholy or homesick. A few guys cried. Everyone but me. I had no one back home.

"Then they opened their care packages while we listened to a broadcast Christmas message from President Johnson. After the service, the chaplain gave everyone a Bible. It was the only present I got."

He looked over at me. "Two days later we were called up to search a small village in Quang Tri.

"It was half an hour before dawn. We were moving in through a rice paddy when a dog started barking. An old man walked out of his hut. He looked around for a moment, then he saw one of our men. I was just ten yards away and I could see it all. The old man and the soldier just stood there staring at each other. Then the old man started shouting.

"That's when all hell broke loose. A dozen machine guns shredded everything in sight. Flame throwers belched out hell. People were screaming and crying." He looked at me. "People were dying.

"Afterward I was counting casualties when I came across a Vietnamese woman huddled near the edge of the jungle. She was holding her son." William's voice suddenly choked with emotion. "He was no older than Dylan. He had been shot and his life was bleeding out on his mother. For a moment we just looked at each other. There was such fear in her eyes. Then she lifted her hand. I thought she had a grenade, so I shot her." His eyes welled up. "When I went to check her for weapons, I found that she was only trying to show me a prayer book."

"I'm sorry," I said.

He slowly shook his head. "Everything about that war was a mess. The brass couldn't figure out how to decide who was winning, so someone decided to measure success by body count. We were being pushed by a general they called the 'Butcher of the Delta.' His ambition was indiscriminate. He ordered the killing of innocent men, women, and children and counted skulls as trophies. He had a saying: 'If it's dead and Vietnamese, it's VC.'

"Four days after leveling that village, on New Year's Eve, we walked into an ambush. Half our platoon was killed. Friends of mine were killed." He looked into my eyes.

"That's when I was taken captive." He looked at me, his eyes revealing his pain.

"You've told me nothing that makes me respect you less," I said. I leaned over and kissed him on the cheek. "Tell me what it was like being a prisoner of war."

"Horror."

"Tell me."

He rubbed his face. "It was day-to-day survival. There was constant physical and mental torture. Worst of all was the unknowing. They wanted us to believe that we might never go home—that no one knew where we were or that they thought we were dead.

"The first year I was tied up in a bamboo cage in the jungle with eleven other men. Six of them died of disease or starvation. After a year or so, those of us who had survived were moved to Hanoi.

"I spent the next few years lying on a bamboo mat on a concrete floor with my legs bound. There were meat hooks hanging from the ceiling above us." His voice softened with the recollection. "That's where I got those scars on my back."

I rubbed his hand.

"We suffered from constant hunger on the edge of starvation. When they did feed us, it was usually old bread and watery soup filled with rat droppings.

"I woke every day in horror. They forced us to speak betrayal, while we struggled to defend something no one fully understood. They told us about the atrocities and corruption going on in South Vietnam. They didn't have to make up lies; they just read to us from the US newspapers.

"The South Vietnamese leaders were gorging themselves off their own people and country. They turned their own people against them. And we were there fighting to hold up one corrupt regime after another in the name of freedom.

"When our government officials lodged complaints over their treatment of their own people, they were told it wasn't any of their business. They'd take our blood and weapons, but not our counsel. We were so afraid of the world turning communist . . . The choice was between one devil or the other."

"You were a pawn in an evil game," I said. "Just like my husband. You paid for their sins. The sin will be on their heads." I looked into his eyes. "Come here."

He leaned forward. I cupped the back of his head and pulled it against my breast and held him while he cried. "I love you," I said.

He pressed himself into me. "I love you too," he said softly.

❆

William and I arrived back at my duplex after dark. There were more snowmen in the yard. Nearly a dozen. Maybe more.

When we went inside Fran was sitting at the table studying. Dylan was already asleep in bed.

"Did you have a good night?" I asked.

Fran nodded. "We watched Disney."

"And made snowmen," I added.

"Yes, we did," Fran said. "Hundreds."

I laughed. "Looks like it."

"Do you need anything else?"

I shook my head. "No. Thank you."

"You're welcome." She looked at William and smiled. "Have a good night."

"You too," William said. "Thanks for watching Dylan."

"Always my pleasure."

After she left I invited William to stay. I felt the need to stay close to him. He was vulnerable and I didn't want him going home alone. I had him lie down on the couch. I put a warm washcloth on his face, then gently massaged his feet.

He fell asleep in our front room around midnight. I didn't try to wake him.

The first week of December passed slowly. Scientists say that time is relative. I believe this. In fact, I created my own formula: $V = D^2 + W$. Time's Velocity = Current Drudgery^2 + the next Worthwhile Event in our life.

Restaurants always pick up around the holidays, so we

all worked as much as we could. William was busy as well but we saw each other when we could. He'd either come by for dinner or, if he worked too late, coffee.

I was excited to spend some real time alone with him again. The next thing on our calendar was the Noel Street Christmas Festival.

CHAPTER

twenty-five

Something happened tonight at the Christmas Festival that I can't explain.

—Elle Sheen's Diary

SATURDAY, DECEMBER 6

For some streets, decorating for Christmas is like putting lipstick on a pig. But Noel Street didn't just share a holiday name, it was made for it. Dickens-era streetlamps with deep green patinas lined the cobblestone street, hung with great pine wreaths. Silver tinsel wires were strung across the width of the road and wrapped with red-and-green ribbon and blinking white and gold lights. In the center of each strand were three-foot-tall silver bells.

The old brick buildings that lined Noel Street still had their original wood-framed glass picture windows, which the local proprietors dressed inside and out, reminiscent of the days when a child could stand on the sidewalk gazing at a magical, sparkling display filled with Christmas dreams.

The street's decorations were the largest line item on the town budget, which was something the locals were proud of. The cynical of heart might write it all off to commercialization, but it was far more than that. It was magic and enchantment. Noel was a street made to be dressed.

The north end of Noel Street—the opposite end of town from the Harrison—circled Garfield Park, a grassy public square with an old wood pavilion and its centerpiece, a massive hundred-and-fifty-year-old Norway spruce. The park was where the festival was held, with the Noel Street traffic flowing into it like a river into a lake.

The Noel Street Christmas Festival was the kind of event that didn't know its potential when it started. In fact, its evolution was so natural that there was an ongoing argument among the locals about who had started it and when it actually began.

There were watermarks along its path. You could say it began sometime in the early fifties when the Downtown Merchants' Association—consisting of less than a dozen business owners—decided to petition the Mistletoe city council to decorate the large spruce. Just a year earlier someone had suggested that the tree should be donated to Rockefeller Center in New York City and almost found themselves run out of town.

With promised donations and the loan of a cherry picker, the council approved the request and the tree was decorated. Just a week later the local elementary school music teacher, Mrs. Carter (who has since passed away), decided to form the Noel Street Chorale, a hodgepodge of singers who met by the tree each weekend night during the holiday season to sing Christmas carols.

At first it was just the singers; then their families came, followed by strangers looking for entertainment in a small town with few amusements. One night, someone had the idea to bring a container of hot cocoa for the singers, a simple act of goodness that led to an unexpected proliferation. By the next year both the size of the chorale group and its audience had doubled and the local women's auxiliary set up a small but permanent stand serving hot cocoa and coffee—not just for the singers but for their audience as well—as a means to raise funds for their local service projects.

Nothing spurs success like profit, and the next year there was another stand selling homemade bread with honey butter. This was followed two weeks later by a donut stand and Mrs. Bench selling hand-knit Christmas stockings and Christmas tree ornaments her husband carved by hand from olive tree wood.

As the park's crowds grew, the members of the original Downtown Merchants' Association realized they had created something perennial, so they again petitioned the city council and reserved the square for an annual Christmas event. A committee was formed and one of the wealthier Mistletoe benefactors visited the famous Christkindlmarkt in Germany and brought back an entire notebook of ideas to bring to the small Mistletoe festival—some practical, some not.

As the Christmas festival grew, it began attracting the citizens of neighboring places, first from the small border towns of Wilden and Tremonton, then eventually drawing those from the larger cities of Ogden, Layton, and Logan.

Soon the festival filled the park and spilled out onto the neighboring streets. It was the only time of year in Mistletoe that open parking spaces weren't a given.

By 1975 the Noel Street Christmas Festival was a complicated affair with bureaucratic regulations and oversight, rented booths, merchant stalls, choir stands, a public address system, and a printed program with two weeks of scheduled performances. Vendors, now coming from outside Mistletoe, sold everything from mulled wine and baked apples to funnel cake and roasted nuts.

There was both a gingerbread house contest, sponsored by the local credit union, and a crèche display, a life-sized nativity with a real donkey and oxen, a stall of reindeer, and, of course, a huge golden throne that Santa himself (accompanied by an enterprising local photographer) inhabited weekend evenings before Christmas.

Dylan had waited all week for the evening, each day building in anticipation like Christmas. Like Christmas, he had trouble sleeping the night before.

William picked us up a little after sundown and we drove downtown, parking in one of the reserved parking places behind the diner. Then the three of us wandered up and down the crowded sidewalks, stopping to watch street performers and carolers and peruse the vendors' booths and sample their wares. Christmas music blared from every corner.

"I can't believe there are this many people," I said, pressing our way through the crowds. "The festival just keeps growing."

"People are looking for something," William said.

We stopped at a booth selling German delicacies and ate bratwurst and sauerkraut sandwiches (something I could never have gotten Dylan to eat on my own) and Spätzle (ditto) with large cups of cider served in plastic steins.

After we'd eaten, we made our way to the crowded square, holding hands with Dylan in the middle. We stopped to take pictures by the Christmas tree and then walked to the main pavilion to listen to a barbershop quartet sing "God Rest Ye Merry, Gentlemen" followed by "It's Beginning to Look a Lot Like Christmas."

"This is impressive," William said. "There are a lot of people here. I wonder where they're coming from."

"It used to just be the locals and couples on dates," I said. "Now look at all the families. They're coming from all over."

We were standing near a large box or crate wrapped in Mylar and tied with a bow to look like a Christmas present. We could see our reflection in the box. Just then Dylan looked up at me with a large smile. "Look, Mama. We're a family."

I smiled back at him, then looked over at William. To my surprise he wasn't smiling. There was a peculiar look in his eyes. He suddenly released Dylan's hand. "Hey, buddy. Want some caramel corn?"

"Yeah."

Dylan hadn't noticed William's nuanced response, but I had. William left us for a moment, then came back with a large bag of caramel corn. From that moment on, William was different. Quieter and disconnected. He was also holding something so he couldn't hold hands. I puzzled to understand what had happened.

It was still early, just a little before nine when William said, "We probably shouldn't keep Dylan up too late."

"You want to go already?" I asked.

"It would probably be best."

I hid my disappointment. "All right," I said. We walked against the flow of a still-growing crowd back to his truck. It was a little after nine o'clock when we arrived back at my duplex. I sent Dylan inside to get ready for bed, remaining outside with William.

"Would you like to come in?" I asked.

"Thanks," he said. "But I'm a little tired."

I took his hand. "Are you okay?"

"I'm fine."

I looked into his eyes. "Are *we* okay?"

The pause after my question was answer enough. "We're fine," he said.

I just looked at him, still unable to read what had happened. Whatever it was, he clearly didn't want to talk about it.

I took a deep breath, then exhaled. "All right. Good night." I stood on my toes to kiss him. He gave me just a light peck on the lips. "Good night."

He turned to go.

"Call me tomorrow?" I asked.

"Sure."

The next day William didn't call or stop by the diner. I knew something had bothered him the previous night. As much as I wanted to see him, I didn't reach out to him. Whatever he was dealing with he needed to work out. But it wasn't easy. My heart ached. It didn't help that in the days leading up to the school Christmas concert, Dylan asked me at least a dozen times if William was going to be there. I wished I knew.

CHAPTER

twenty-six

To have children is, by necessity, to be vulnerable.
—Elle Sheen's Diary

FRIDAY, DECEMBER 12

The morning of the big program my heart wrestled with the competing emotions of excitement and dread. *I still haven't heard from William since the festival. Where is he?*

Dylan was over-the-top excited about the concert and his debut performance as a first-grade bell ringer. It was a really big deal for him, which only made me more anxious about not hearing from William. Notwithstanding, I didn't want anything to take away from Dylan's day.

I put chocolate chips in his Cream of Wheat, something reserved for very special occasions, then dressed him in red corduroy pants with a long-sleeved white cotton shirt and green suspenders.

"You, little man, look like Christmas personified," I said. "Santa would be proud."

"Is Santa going to be there?" he asked.

"I don't think so."

"Is Mr. William going to be there?"

I deflected the question. "We'll see. Are you ready to ring that bell?"

He nodded. "I practiced."

Only seven kids in the entire school got to play an instrument; a fifth-grade boy who played the drum during "The Little Drummer Boy," three third-grade girls who played plastic recorders during "Silent Night," then the three children in Dylan's class who got to ring bells for "Jingle Bells." The rest of the children were assigned to general chorus duty.

As I put on his coat, Dylan asked, "Is Mr. William picking us up?"

"No. He's coming from work. We're going to meet him there."

His little forehead furrowed. "Is he coming for sure?"

My heart ached at the question. "I don't know for sure. He said he was coming. Unless there's an emergency at work, he'll be there."

"I hope there's not an emergency," Dylan replied. "This is a pretty big deal."

I still love that he said that.

Dylan and I got in the car. I started it up and turned on the heater. There was a huge burst of air, then nothing.

"No, no, no," I said.

"What's wrong, Mama?" Dylan asked.

I groaned. "This car hates me."

To my huge relief (and surprise), William was waiting for us at the school when we got there. Dylan picked out his truck in the school parking lot the moment we drove in. I didn't know where he'd been but at that moment, I really didn't care. I was just glad he was there. I just didn't want to see Dylan disappointed on such an important day.

William must have gotten there pretty early because he'd secured front-row seats for us. As usual, most of those in attendance were mothers and grandparents with a sprinkling of fathers who could get off work. William looked a little out of place. He was taller and younger than most and decidedly male. He was also dressed nicely, nothing he'd be wearing to work at Renato's.

I sent Dylan to his classroom and then walked up to the front of the little auditorium. It had been decorated for the concert with a few hundred snowflakes the children had cut out.

William stood when he saw me. "Hi," he said. Noticeably, he didn't try to kiss me.

"Thanks so much for coming," I said. "Dylan asked me at least a half dozen times if you were going to be here."

"I wouldn't miss it for the world," he said.

We sat down together. "How have you been?" I asked.

He avoided my gaze. "Just busy, you know?"

"I know," I said. I looked at him. "I've missed you."

"I've missed you too," he said softly.

"Did I do something wrong?"

He looked down, threading his fingers together. "No." Then he reached over and took my hand. For the moment I let it go at that. I wanted his touch. I didn't want to spoil anything.

Fran arrived a few minutes before the concert. William hadn't known she was coming, and all the seats around us were taken, so she said hello, then went and sat near the back of the room.

The concert started promptly at nine thirty. Howard Taft Elementary School was small, with less than two hundred students in seven grades. The kindergarteners went first, which was more an exercise in herding cats than a musical performance. They were singing "Rudolph, the Red-Nosed Reindeer" and someone had the bright idea of putting red noses—foam rubber clown noses, really—on each of the kids. Needless to say, the whole song (to the delight of photograph-snapping adults) was just an exercise in children chasing little red balls across the floor.

After the teachers had collected the noses, the next performance was Dylan's class with "Jingle Bells." The kids sang loudly and happily, and Dylan, who was taking the bell thing way too seriously, rang his bell with stoic concentration, his eyes not once leaving his teacher, Mrs. Duncan, who was directing the song.

We endured another four songs, and then William and I joined the rest of the parents in the cafeteria for milk and frosted Christmas-tree-shaped sugar cookies.

I was looking around for Dylan when I noticed him on the other side of the cafeteria with a group of children. He was pointing toward us.

"I'll be right back," I said to William. I crossed the room, smiling like only a proud mother could. "You were so great," I said when I got to him. "You really rang that bell."

Dylan just looked at me with a peculiar expression, the kind he wore when I caught him doing something he wasn't supposed to be doing.

Just then, Mrs. Duncan walked up to me. "Hi, Elle."

"Congratulations," I said. "That was awesome."

"Congratulations to you," she returned.

I smiled. "For what?"

"Dylan tells us he's getting a father." She looked across the room at William. "Is that the lucky man?"

Dylan looked at me sheepishly.

"Mr. Smith is only a friend," I said. I looked at Dylan, unsure how to respond. I was torn between making him apologize and just holding him.

Just then one of the boys said, "I told you he was lying."

Dylan ran out of the room.

"Sorry," I said to his teacher. I chased after him. I found him hiding behind a row of coats in his classroom. I squatted down next to him. "Are you okay?"

He just looked at me with tears in his eyes.

"I'm not going to get mad at you." I breathed out heavily, then sat down on the floor. "You know, it's hard not having a father, isn't it?"

He slowly nodded.

"You may not know it, but we're in the same boat, you and I. I don't have a father either. Sometimes I even cry about it. It doesn't seem fair, does it?"

He shook his head.

"You need to know something. You have a father. And he was a really great man. A special man. Your father is a hero. But you never got to see him, and that's not very fair to you. But he loved you very much, and he was so excited about coming home from the war and seeing you. He was excited about playing baseball and going tubing and taking you camping." My eyes welled up.

"But that didn't get to happen. I'm so sorry. And I know that he's sorry. But *you* have nothing to be sorry about. Because you're just a wonderful little boy in a big world, and none of this is your fault. Not one little bit. Do you understand that? You have nothing to be sorry or embarrassed about."

Dylan's eyes welled up too.

"Mr. William likes you very, very much. He's not your father, but he still cares about you and me, and that's a good thing. The other day he told me what a great kid you are. Do you know what I told him?"

Dylan shook his head again.

"I told him that he was right, that you're the best kid I know. But whether or not you ever have a father doesn't change that one little bit.

"And you know what? Someday you might have the chance to *be* a father. And that little boy or girl will be the luckiest person in the whole world except for me, because I'll always be luckier. Because you're my son, and I'm awfully glad I got to be your mother."

For a moment Dylan just looked at me. Then he came out from behind the coats into my arms. I just held him. "I love you, my little man. I love you with all my heart."

CHAPTER

twenty-seven

This afternoon, William . . .
[I never finished writing this entry. Next to those words
there was just the stain of two teardrops. I suppose that
says more than I could have written.]

—Elle Sheen's Diary

After a few more minutes I said, "Do you feel better?"
He nodded.

"Would you like to get a cookie?"

He nodded again.

I leaned back and kissed his forehead. "Okay. Let's go."

I held his hand as we walked back down the hall to the cafeteria. The crowd had cleared a little but there were still dozens of children swarming around the cookie table.

"Do you want me to go with you?" I asked.

"No, thank you."

"Okay. I'll be over here with Mr. William." I let go of his hand and he ran over to the cookies where the other children were.

I looked around for William, hoping that he hadn't left.

I found him standing alone on the south side of the cafeteria, leaning against the wall. I walked over to him.

"Where have you been?" he asked. Frankly, I wanted to ask him the same question.

"I had to talk to Dylan. He was telling some of the other children that you're his father."

William looked at me with a peculiar expression. "What?"

"Don't worry, I told him to stop."

William's expression turned still harder. He looked upset. "Why would he do that?"

The intensity of his response surprised me. "Why are you so upset by this? You should be flattered. Dylan looks up to you. He just wanted to be like the other kids whose dads are here."

William didn't say anything.

"Are you telling me that it's never even crossed your mind?"

"Has what crossed my mind?" he said angrily.

My eyes welled up. I covered them with my hand. "Oh my gosh." My pain turned to anger. I looked up at him. "What's going on? Why haven't you called?"

"I told you."

"You told me nothing!" I shouted. I noticed all the other parents looking at us. "Come outside."

William followed me outside the school. I turned on him. "What is this?"

"What is what?"

"This . . . us."

"What did you think this was?"

"Clearly not what you did," I said.

"Did I ever tell you that I was looking for a relationship?"

"Not in words."

"I didn't come to this place to fall in love."

I looked at him for a moment, then said, "But you did, didn't you?"

He didn't answer.

"That's what it is, isn't it?" When he didn't answer I said, "You came here for whatever reason and fell in love and you got scared."

"What do you know about being scared?" he said.

I caught my breath. My head was spinning. "Maybe nothing compared to you. But what I know is that you went through a hell that few people could understand and you had every reason to die yet you fought to live. And now that you're back, you're afraid of living."

"What do I have to live for?"

The question stung. "I thought I was something to live for. I thought Dylan was something to live for."

He didn't speak. The rejection that burned in me turned to anger. "You're a coward. You're not afraid of death, you're afraid that life might be worth living. You're afraid you might have to forgive yourself."

"There is no such thing as forgiveness."

"That's not true."

"Really? Have you forgiven your father?"

Again, his words stung. I couldn't answer.

"Have you forgiven yourself for sending Isaac to fight in

a war he didn't believe in and never came back from? Have you forgiven yourself for sending him to his death?"

His words sent a shock through me. My knees weakened. I began to tremble. "I didn't send him to his death."

"Are you sure?"

The words were like a spear through my heart. At first I couldn't breathe. William stood there helplessly. Suddenly Fran walked out of the school. She looked at me, breathless and heaving in pain, and walked over. "Oh, honey. What happened?" She spun toward William. "What did you do to her?"

William just stood there.

"What did you do to her?!" she screamed.

He just stood there awkwardly and speechless. When I caught my breath, I looked up at him and said softly, "If I tell you you're right, will you leave me?"

"I'm so sorry," he said.

I couldn't stop shaking. "Please."

"You need to leave," Fran said. "You need to leave now."

He just looked at me, his eyes welling. "I'm really sorry." He turned and walked away.

After several minutes Fran said, "It's cold, Elle. Let's get you inside."

"I don't want to go inside. I don't want Dylan to see me like this."

Fran took my hand. "I understand. Let me walk you to the car, then I'll get Dylan. I'll take him to my place."

"All right," I said softly.

We walked together across the wet pavement to my car. Fran opened my door, hugged me, and then helped me in.

"Are you sure you can drive?"

I nodded.

"Okay. Just call when you want me to bring him back. He can spend the night if you want."

"Thank you."

She stood there looking at me with sympathetic eyes. Then she said, "What do you want me to tell Dylan if he asks about William?"

"Tell him he's gone."

CHAPTER

twenty-eight

How is it that we don't see the train until we're beneath it?
                                              —Elle Sheen's Diary

Dylan slept that night at Fran's. I couldn't sleep. I tried. I even took sleeping pills, anything to escape the pain, but nothing helped.

As I tossed in bed, somewhere in the middle of the night, something hit me. Something William had said at the school that stole any hope I had of sleep. *Did he really say what I thought he said?*

I waited until the sun came up, then, in just my sweats and a T-shirt, I put on my coat and drove to Renato's.

William's truck wasn't in the parking lot. I stormed into the repair shop's lobby. Renato was there talking to some man. They both turned and looked at me. Without speaking, I opened the door to the garage. No one was there.

I turned back to Renato. "Where is he?" I asked. "Where's William?"

Renato looked at me sadly. "William quit. He said he had to move on."

The words felt like a brick on my chest. "When?"

"He came by my house last night."

"Did he already leave?"

"I don't know," he said. "He was very upset."

I ran back out to my car. I had to see him. I had to know the truth. I drove to the Harrison with tears running down my cheeks. To my relief, William's truck was still there.

I ran upstairs and pounded on his door. It was nearly a full minute before William opened it. He said nothing, his gaze locked on mine.

"I never told you my husband's name," I said. "I never told you his name was Isaac. You knew him, didn't you? You knew my husband."

William just looked at me.

"Tell me!" I shouted. "You knew my husband!"

William's face showed neither anger nor indifference. After a moment he said, "Come in."

His apartment looked even barer than before, if that was possible. There were two large green canvas duffel bags on the floor next to the couch. There was a gun on top of one of the bags.

William sat at one end of the couch. "Have a seat," he said softly.

I sat at the other end of the couch. I just sat there, trembling.

William rubbed his chin and said, "I knew Isaac. He was my best friend. I was with him when he died."

My eyes welled up.

"It was that New Year's Eve I told you about, right after the attack on Quang Tri. Our platoon walked into an ambush. Isaac got hit right off. I carried him to some rocks next to a waterfall, but he was bleeding badly. I needed to get him out of there, but we were pinned down. We were outnumbered. The bullets were thicker than mosquitoes." The pain and fear in his eyes was fresh, as if he were reliving the moment.

"I kept telling him to hang in there, that we were going to make it. But we both knew otherwise." William swallowed. "His last thoughts were of you. He was afraid you would blame yourself for his death. He was afraid of his son growing up without a father. He asked me to find you and tell you that he loved you."

William's eyes welled up. "I was carrying him when I was captured." He looked into my eyes. "You wanted to know what kept me alive through that hell? It was that promise." He closed his eyes tight, forcing a tear down his cheek. "Actually there were two promises. He made me promise to give you something." He breathed out slowly. "I was going to mail it to you after I left."

He reached into one of the duffel bags and brought out a black velvet pouch. "You have no idea what it took to get this to you." He handed it to me.

I opened the pouch and poured its contents into my palm. It was Isaac's wedding band. I looked up at William.

"I swallowed it at least a hundred times to keep them from finding it. If they had seen me swallow it, they would have cut me open."

I looked at the ring, caressing it between my fingers. It was just a simple gold band, all we could afford at the time. I remembered slipping it on Isaac's finger. William had risked his life to bring it to me.

"When I came back to America, I realized that the promise I made to Isaac was the only thing that kept me alive."

"Then he gave you a gift," I said.

He shook his head. "It was a curse." He looked at me. "You asked me why I came to Mistletoe. I came to fulfill a promise to my friend and then do what I should have done back in Vietnam."

"What's that?"

"Die."

The word echoed in my heart. "That place you took me," I said. "The falls . . ."

"That was where I was going to take my life."

"That's why you were crying?"

"I was crying because I was carrying Isaac like that when he died."

I let the words sink in. "Why did it take you so long to find me?"

"I was a mess. I was trying to make something stick. I couldn't."

"Maybe it was the wrong thing you were trying to make stick. Maybe God had something better for you."

"There is no God."

"Then why are you so angry at Him?"

He didn't answer. For a long time there was only silence.

"I don't know why I didn't see it before, but I understand now," I said. "You were afraid because you finally found a family. You found what was taken from you all those years ago."

He put his head down. I moved closer to him. I reached out and touched his cheek. He raised his head to look at me.

"Can't you see it? This is too big a coincidence. Have you considered that maybe Isaac didn't ask you to make that promise for him? That promise was for *you*. It kept you alive through that hell. It brought you to us. He gave you a gift. He gave you back a family. He gave you us."

"That's what I'm afraid of."

"It's not what you're afraid of," I said. "It's what you're afraid of losing. Why else would you have come here and taken an apartment and a job. You could have just found me at the diner and left the same day.

"William, God is giving you this. He's giving you a second chance. But you have to have the courage to take it. It's your choice now. You can have what you've always wanted. I know you're afraid of losing us. After all you've been through, who wouldn't be? But this time, this moment, is up to you but if you don't take the chance, you've already lost us."

William was quiet for the longest time, thinking, searching. The whole time I silently prayed, hoping he would have faith just one more time—hoping that he would believe. Then he looked up at me. I knew his answer before he spoke. All he said was "I'm sorry."

His words ended the conversation. My heart knew it

was over. We were over. "Me too," I said. After a minute I took a deep breath. I felt nothing but darkness. "Are you going to take your life?"

"I don't know."

"Please don't. Not that what I think matters." I looked him in the eyes. "I love you, William. More than I could ever say." I swallowed. "And I know you love me."

He looked at me for a moment, then said, "More than I've ever loved anyone or anything." Then he said something I'll never forget. "It's the only thing more terrifying than death."

"That's the price of love," I said. "The risk of losing it. But it's worth the risk."

"Is it?"

I took another deep breath. "I guess that's for you to decide."

I just sat there for a moment. Then I wiped my eyes and lifted the golden ring. "Thank you for this." I stood. "I guess I better let you get on with your life."

As he stood, I walked over and put my arms around him, my head against his chest. With his arms around me, he pulled me in close. For just a moment I pretended that this was something else, but my heart wouldn't allow it. I stepped back, kissed him, then turned and walked out of his life.

CHAPTER

twenty-nine

Broken hearts tend to take the rest of the body with them.
                                    —Elle Sheen's Diary

It was only a week until Christmas. I was alone. Dylan had been with Fran for two days.

I couldn't stand the sound of my thoughts, so I turned on the radio to one of those all-Christmas-all-the-time stations. "I Heard the Bells on Christmas Day" by Harry Belafonte played.

There is no peace on earth, I said to myself. *Never has been. Never will be.* The phrase from the song clung to my heart like a burr.

My heart was broken.

Most of all I was tired. Tired of loneliness and responsibility. And, in spite of my exhaustion, I could see no respite, no reprieve, no way out, and Christmas was looming ahead of me like an iceberg in the path of a titanic meltdown.

Dylan would be back soon. I wished I had someone to send him off with for a while. Fran would have kept him for as long as I needed, but she was leaving town for the holidays. I couldn't hide my brokenness.

My thoughts were interrupted by the doorbell. It was Gretchen, my landlady. The sight of her just made my stomach hurt more. She stood on the porch holding a plate of cookies. She looked at me, clearly shocked by my appearance. My hair was a rat's nest, and I had no makeup on. I hadn't worn makeup for days.

"Elle, are you . . . okay?"

"I've been better," I said. "Come in."

She stepped inside. "Are you sick?"

"No."

"Is it the window?" she asked. "You know they caught that evil woman."

"This has just been a hard month. It's been a hard year."

"I'm really sorry." She forced a smile. "But cheer up. I brought you my famous pepperkaker cookies. The ones that sell like hotcakes at the festival. They're always good for a smile."

"Thank you," I said. I took the plate from her and set it down on the table. I turned back. "Look, I know I'm late on rent, but . . . is there any way we could split this month across the next three months."

Gretchen looked confused. "You want to split up your rent?"

"Just for the next three months," I said. "I think I can get back on track."

"I'm sure I don't know what you're talking about."

"My rent," I said, angry that she was making my request more difficult than it already was. "You came here to collect the rent, right?"

She looked even more confused. "No, I came to bring you cookies. Your rent's paid."

"I don't understand."

"Honey, there's nothing to understand. Your rent is paid up to the end of next year, which I am very grateful for."

"You must be mistaken. I didn't pay it."

"Not you, dear. It was the man you sent."

"What man?"

"The one you sent with your rent. I've never met him before. He told me he was paying the bill for you. He paid in cash."

I let the news sink in. "Was his name William?"

She bit her lip. "I'm sorry, he didn't give me his name. He was a nice-looking gent, older, maybe in his late fifties."

"Fifties? Are you sure?"

"Oh yes. He had fabulous gray hair."

I honestly had no idea who it could be.

"I assumed you knew." She smiled. "Maybe it was someone you met at the diner." She raised her eyebrows. "Maybe you have a secret admirer."

"I don't know anyone who could have done that."

She shrugged. "Well, someone paid it. Maybe it was an angel. Maybe it's a Christmas miracle. I'm happy for you, Elle. You deserve a break. Maybe this news will brighten your day a little. Or a lot. Merry Christmas, my dear."

"Merry Christmas to you too," I said.

I shut the door after her. *Who had paid my rent?*

CHAPTER

thirty

I had an unexpected visitor today.

        —Elle Sheen's Diary

Fran came by with Dylan a little after seven o'clock. She honked "shave and a haircut" as she pulled into my driveway—something Dylan always made her do. She was on her way to Texas to visit her family, and the back seat of her car was full of wrapped gifts and suitcases.

The passenger-side door opened and Dylan practically sprang from it, running to me and shouting, "Mama! Mama! I missed you!" I hugged him tight and kissed the top of his head. "I missed you too, buddy."

He stood back. "Look!" He held out a wrapped box. "Fran gave me a present. But she says I can't open it until Christmas."

"Go put it under the tree," I said. "I'll be right there."

He ran into the house. Fran walked up to me, leaving her car idling.

"He's had a bath and I fed him dinner." She looked at me. "Elle, I'm so sorry I can't keep him longer. You know I would."

"You've done more than enough. I'm worried about you driving at night. Are you sure you won't wait until morning?"

"I'll be okay. I'm just going to Green River tonight, maybe Laramie if the roads aren't too bad. That's not too far."

"I'm sorry I delayed your trip. But I don't know what I would have done without you."

"I think that about you all the time," she said. "And my buddy Dylan. You're my family too. I'll be back January third, okay? I'll plan on getting right back into it." She leaned forward and we hugged. "Merry Christmas, Elle. Nineteen seventy-six will be a better year. I promise. You know I'm right about these things. It's the psychic in me."

"I'm going to hold you to that," I said, forcing a smile for her. "Merry Christmas."

"I love you," she said.

"And I love you."

She walked back to her car. I shut the door behind her. I walked over to the tree. Dylan was sitting next to it. "How was your visit with Fran?" I asked.

"I can't wait to see what she got me. Is Mr. William coming for Christmas?"

"No. Mr. William had to go away."

"For . . . ever?"

"Yes."

Dylan looked sad. "But I like him."

A tear fell down my cheek. I made no attempt to hide it. "Me too, buddy. Me too."

An hour later there was a knock at my door. I had already sent Dylan to bed, and I guessed it might be Fran coming back. Maybe she had decided to wait to leave until tomorrow after all. I opened the door, ready to give her a big hug.

My father stood in the doorway.

CHAPTER

thirty-one

One cannot understand the power of grace until one has needed it. Or given it.

—Elle Sheen's Diary

I didn't recognize him at first. He was older, of course, but he looked older than I would have thought after six years. He was completely gray, the hair at the top of his head thinning. Maybe it was because I no longer feared him, but he seemed smaller and softer somehow, even though he still held himself like a military man.

"Hi, Miche," he said. He pronounced it "Meesh." Michelle was my real name, but everyone except my father called me by the abbreviated *Elle*.

For a long time I was speechless. Finally I asked, "How did you find me?"

"A mutual friend."

"We don't have mutual friends."

He cleared his throat. "Seeing me is probably a pretty big shock."

"That's an understatement," I said.

Just then Dylan walked up behind me. "Mama." I didn't want him to see my father, but it was too late. He stood behind me staring. Then he said, "I'm Dylan. Who are you?"

"Don't tell him," I said.

My father glanced at me, then back at Dylan. "You can call me Larry."

"Hi, Mr. Larry," Dylan said.

"Dylan, I need you to go back to your room."

Dylan frowned, then stomped back to his room.

"I'm sorry it's so late," my father said. "I tried to catch you earlier, but you weren't at the diner."

"How do you know where I work?"

"Same friend," he said. "May I please come in? I promise I won't stay long."

I didn't move. I think I felt that letting him in was, in some way, symbolic of letting him back into my life, something that wasn't going to happen.

"Just five minutes and I'll be gone," he said.

I thought over his request. "All right. But just five minutes."

"Five minutes," he echoed. "Thank you."

I stepped back from the door and let him in. I walked to my kitchen and brought out an egg timer. I set it for five minutes, then put it on the table. My father watched my demonstration but said nothing about it.

"You have a nice place. May I sit down?"

I nodded. I noticed he was holding a brown manila envelope under his arm. For a moment we just looked at each other without speaking.

"You don't have much time."

"I know . . . It's just been so long." He glanced at the

egg timer, breathed in deeply, then sighed. "I came to tell you that I'm sorry. What I did to you, especially at such a difficult time, was unconscionable. I am ashamed of what I did. I don't expect you to forgive me, but I wanted you to know that I'm sorry. I was wrong."

It was the first time I had heard those words come out of his mouth. It should have felt good, but it didn't. I read somewhere that we always react angrily at people for finally doing what they should have done before. I wanted to punish him.

"Wrong about what?" I said.

"Pretty much everything," he said. He looked down.

"What were you hoping would come from this?" I said. "That after all this time I was just going to let you back into our lives? Is that what you expected?"

He continued looking down, the balding crown of his head showing. "Expected? No." He slowly looked up. "But I was hoping."

I didn't respond.

"I believe that when you repent, you need to make restitution, when possible. I wanted to see if you'd let me make up for what I should have done a long time ago."

"Is that what this is? Repentance?"

"In part."

I suddenly understood. "You paid my rent."

He nodded. The bell rang on the egg timer. I glanced down at it and then back at him. "What made you think I wanted your help?"

"I didn't think you wanted my help. I just thought you probably needed it."

I wasn't sure how to respond to that. He glanced down at his watch. "Well, I've taken my five minutes. Thank you for hearing me out. I'm sorry to bother you. I just wanted to tell you in person how sorry I am." He slowly stood, his gaze catching mine. "And how much I've missed my girl." His eyes were moist. "I've made some big mistakes in my life, Miche, but none bigger than my mistake with you. Turning away my only daughter is unforgivable. I hope you can forgive me someday. Not for my sake—I don't deserve it—but yours. For your own peace."

William's words about forgiving my father echoed back to me.

My father turned toward the door and began walking toward it. "What I want doesn't matter, anyway. At least not for much longer."

"What do you mean by that?" I said.

He didn't answer, but continued toward the door.

"What did you mean by 'much longer'?"

He turned back and looked at me as if he were trying to decide whether or not to answer. "I have cancer, Miche. The doctors say I won't be around much longer."

The words affected me more than I wanted them to. "That's why you came back now? Guilt? Dying regrets?"

He looked at me sadly. "No, the guilt and regret were there long before the cancer. Up until now I didn't know where you were." He gazed into my eyes. "I've looked for you for years. I even hired a private eye, but he failed. I had no idea where you went. I didn't even know what your new last name was. For all I knew you had left the country." He sighed. "I'd given up hope of ever seeing you again until your friend showed up."

"Who is this friend?" I asked.

"Second Lieutenant Smith."

It took me a moment to understand. "You saw . . . William?"

He nodded.

The revelation angered me. My life was none of William's business. "What did he tell you?"

"Much," he said softly. He breathed out. "He told me about Isaac—the kind of man he was, the kind of soldier he was. He told me how he was killed in action." My father's voice choked. "I'm so sorry you had to go through that alone. I'm sorry I wasn't there for you."

I could see the pain in his eyes.

"He told me he was ashamed of me."

"What did you say to that?"

"He didn't tell me anything I didn't already believe. I told him that I was ashamed of myself.

"Then he told me about you and Dylan. I asked him whether he thought you'd talk to me if I went to see you. He said he didn't know, but if I had any courage left in me, I should try." He cleared his throat, blinking away the forming tears. "I can't change what I've done, Miche. I can only try to change the future. I came to do the right thing if that's possible." He looked into my eyes. "If you'll let me. I know I'm asking a lot, but it would be a true mercy."

As I looked into his vulnerable, pleading eyes, the man standing before me somehow changed to me. I no longer saw the rigid military man who had rejected my baby and me that painful night. I saw someone different. I saw a humble, broken man mourning the mistakes of his past. I saw a grieving, aging man trying to make something right, not just for him, but for the sake of right itself. I saw through the veil of mistake and circumstance a man I'd once known, a man who had provided and cared for me. A man who had held my hand and carried me on his shoulders when I was tired. A man who, in his own, sometimes flawed ways, always did his best to protect me. In short, I saw my father again.

I couldn't speak for a long time. Then I nodded. "All right."

Those two simple words had a profound impact on him—more, perhaps, than I could understand. He wiped his eyes with his forearm, then took the brown envelope from under his arm and handed it to me. "This is mostly just a lot of legal mumbo jumbo. I set up a college fund for Dylan. There's enough there for his education at a good school, also books and housing. He has several years before then, so the fund should grow a bit. It might even help him get into a house someday."

"You paid for Dylan's college?"

"There's something else. I set up another fund. It's in that same envelope. It's called the Isaac Sheen Scholarship Fund. It's for one Negro student each year at Arizona State."

"Thank you."

"It's long past due," he said.

As I looked into his eyes, I suddenly started crying. He

just stood there, almost at attention, his face full of emotion. "We once had a wonderful relationship, Miche. You were my life. My light. We had such fun." He grinned. "Well, maybe I was never much fun, but I tried."

I laughed through my tears. "You were fun. Sometimes."

He laughed as well. Then his gaze grew more serious. "My sins have brought their own punishment, Miche."

Hearing this made my heart hurt, not just for my loss but my father's as well. I thought of my love for Dylan and understood that my father loved me the same. For the first time I realized just how much he had suffered too.

I wondered if he'd gone through this alone or if my mother had changed as well. "Where's Mom?" I asked.

My father looked down. "She's gone. She tried, but . . ." He cleared his throat. "Two years ago her liver failed. We tried for a transplant, but it was too late."

I suddenly felt my own pain of loss. "I'm sorry I wasn't there for you."

"It was my own fault." His eyes welled up. "I can't tell you how many times I've looked through our photographs of us. The Christmases we spent. I've missed my daughter."

"I've missed you, Dad."

He swallowed. "May I hug you?"

"I would like that." I fell into him and we embraced. It felt so good to be held by him again.

"Thank you, Miche."

"Thank you, Daddy."

After we parted, his eyes were red. "Do you think I

could see Dylan? I won't tell him who I am. I just want to see my grandson."

"Yes." I walked to Dylan's room and opened the door. As I expected, he wasn't asleep. He was always curious when someone new was in the house.

"Dylan. I want you to meet someone."

"Is it Mr. Larry?"

"Yes."

Dylan hopped out of bed. He walked directly up to my father. "Mr. Larry, why are you at my house?"

My father crouched down on his haunches. "I came to see how you and your mother were doing. You are a handsome young man."

"I know," Dylan said. "Who are you again?"

My father just looked at him and then wiped his eyes.

"Why are you crying?" Dylan asked.

"Because I'm sorry you had to ask that."

I stepped forward. "Dylan, this is your grandpa. My father."

Dylan looked puzzled. "You said you didn't have a father."

"I was wrong," I said.

"I have a grandpa?"

"You do," my father said. "I'm right here."

Dylan still looked confused. Then he asked, "Where have you been?"

"I've been lost," he said. "Very, very lost."

"And someone found you?"

He smiled. "Yes. Someone found me. A soldier." He glanced at me, then back to Dylan. "If it's okay with you and your mother, I'd like to invite you to our house for Christmas. I'll even take you on a sleigh ride through the mountain with real horses."

"You have real horses?"

"Yes. And real cows, goats, and chickens."

"Are you a farmer?"

"Yes, I am. And I have a big farmhouse, but no one to spend Christmas with."

Dylan looked at me. "Can we go to his big farmhouse for Christmas, Mama?"

I nodded. "Yes."

I looked over at my father. He didn't even try to stop his tears.

CHAPTER

thirty-two

Throughout history, the homecoming has been celebrated in story and in song. I have never understood why as well as I do today as I celebrate it in my heart.
—Elle Sheen's Diary

Two days later, Dylan and I made the three-hundred-mile drive south to Cedar City. I hadn't been there since I'd left six years earlier. It took us five hours. It's hard to believe that just five hours had separated so much.

I was wearing Isaac's ring on a gold chain around my neck. It was the gold chain my father had given me at my high school graduation. I hadn't worn it since I left, but even in the hard times I hadn't been able to pawn it either. Maybe, like William, I was still holding on to something I couldn't bring myself to admit I wanted. Or needed.

"The old Fairlane," he said, walking out to greet us. "I'm a little surprised it's still running."

"Barely," I said. "I just replaced the alternator, clutch, and timing belt."

His brow furrowed. "What did that set you back?"

"Not as much as it should have," I said. "William fixed

it for free. But it hasn't stopped the rest of it from falling apart." I grinned. "I think it has leprosy."

My father chuckled. "Old cars don't get new."

I smiled. "I've heard that."

❄

Christmas Eve was a giant party. My father had cut his own tree from the forest behind his property. Unlike the small tree at home, his was massive and rose nearly fourteen feet high in his spacious living room, filling the entire room with its beautiful fragrance. It was elaborately decorated with beautiful lights, ribbons, and ornaments.

"Who decorated your tree?" I asked.

He looked at me with surprise. "I did, of course. You know I'm a Christmasphile."

I smiled with remembrance. It was true. My father loved Christmas.

My father had a lot of friends whom he'd invited over to see his returned daughter and grandson. Probably close to a hundred people came by the house. I shouldn't have been surprised, but there were a lot of single, older ladies who spent a lot of time with us. Frankly, I didn't know there were that many single women in Cedar City, but I suppose, for my dad, they were probably coming from other cites as well. There were even a few handsome ranchers that my father, not so discreetly, informed I was single.

At the height of the party my father walked to the center of the room with a glass of wine. He clinked on the glass with a spoon until the room was quiet. "I'd like to make a toast," he said. He turned to me. "As most of you know, Christmas is a special time of year for me. At least it was. There hasn't been a tree in this house since my daughter left. I swore that there would be no tree until she came back. I had begun to lose hope that there would ever be a tree in this house again."

His eyes welled. "But Christmas is about hope. The Wise Men traveled far to find a mother with her child in a simple manger. The same is true for me. I may not be wise, but I was searching. And God, in His infinite goodness, sent me a star to find her. So I raise a toast to that star, a soldier who set me on the right path, I raise a toast to the season itself and its promise of hope. Most of all, I raise a toast to that mother and her beautiful, beautiful child. May Christmas forever live in our hearts." He raised his glass. "To Christmas."

I raised mine and said softly, "And to the Father."

All in all, it was a glorious celebration with food and music, laughter and joy, and I think Dylan had more fun than the rest of us.

After everyone had left, including a few of the women I practically had to shoo away, my father and I stayed up late and told stories of the old days, some true, some not so much. Mostly my father just wanted to know all about my life since I'd left.

In the end he asked about William and what had happened between us. I was surprised at how much I was willing to share. Even though he'd broken my heart, he'd given me a precious gift. He'd given me my father back. And he'd given Dylan a grandfather. Most of all, he'd given my heart something I didn't want to believe was lacking—forgiveness.

"He loves you," he said.

I nodded. "I know. But maybe not enough."

My father nodded, then said, "Don't underestimate the power of love over fear."

My father had prepared my old room upstairs for my return and one across the hall for Dylan. Being in a strange house, I asked Dylan if he wanted to sleep with me—something he often asked to do even in our house—but, for the first time ever, he turned me down. He was pretty excited to have his own room in the farmhouse.

The next morning Dylan and I woke to the smell of coffee and Burl Ives's Christmas music playing from my father's television stereo. It was a powerful flashback for me, reminding me of many happy Christmases we had shared together.

Dylan and I walked downstairs to find the tree literally buried in a mountain of presents. There were more than twenty gifts for each of us. I don't know how my father knew what we wanted, but he did pretty well, though he later confessed that several lady friends had lent a hand in the purchasing and wrapping department.

Throughout the morning's unveilings, my father just sat in his old La-Z-Boy chair, the same one I remembered from my childhood, and watched the proceedings with a joyful smile that practically split his face from one side to the other.

The gifts he gave us were more than extravagant, and Dylan looked like he was living a dream he was afraid to wake up from. He got a cassette tape recorder, a phonograph player system with a built-in 8-track player, Jackson 5 and 5th Dimension albums, a pet rock, and a plethora of other amusements. There was even a new Atari Pong game, the expensive one Dylan sometimes talked about but knew I would never be able to afford. One of his favorite gifts was his own pair of leather cowboy boots.

"Look, Mama, boots!" he said, holding them up. "I'm a cowboy."

"Put them on," I said.

"Can I?" he asked.

"Of course. That's what they're for."

Dylan pulled the boots on over his bare feet.

"Now you look like a real cowboy," I said.

"Except for a hat," my dad said. "Every cowboy needs a hat. Wait a second, I think I got one of those too." From behind the chair he brought out a small felt cowboy hat. He threw the hat to Dylan like it was a Frisbee.

"Wow!" Dylan said. He put it on. Backward.

"Other way, partner," my father said.

Dylan turned it around.

"It's a Stetson. That's the real McCoy."

"That's really too much, Dad."

"No," he said, winking at me. "It's not."

After we'd opened the last present, my father said, "I got one more thing for you, Miche."

"You got me enough already," I replied.

"Now don't be difficult," he said, standing. "It's just one more thing. But try as I might, I couldn't get it through the door, so I left it outside. Come on, Dylan. I have something outside for you too."

"Is mine too big to come in the house too?"

"Well, yours can't come inside for other reasons," he said.

We followed my father out the side door. Sitting beneath the covered driveway was a brand-new cherry-red Valiant.

"It's the Valiant Regal sedan, six-cylinder, four-speed," he said, sounding almost like a TV commercial. "American made, of course. One of Chrysler's best new cars of the year."

"It's beautiful." I hugged my father. "Thank you so much, Dad . . ."

"Is that our new car?" Dylan asked.

"It sure is," I said.

"Can I tell Albert?"

"You can tell anyone you want," I said.

"Open the door, girl," my father said. "Nothing like the smell of a new car."

I opened the door and looked inside. It was gorgeous.

"Can I get in?" Dylan asked.

"Of course."

He jumped inside the front seat, falling back in the bucket seat. He turned to me. "It kind of stinks."

I smiled. "It's the new car smell. You'll learn to like it."

"Have you ever seen a Valiant?" my father asked.

"Funny you should ask. I drove an older model a few weeks ago. While they were fixing the Fairlane." I smiled. "Everyone kept telling me it was sexy."

"Well, I don't know about that, but it's a solid car and brand-spanking new, right off the dealership floor."

"You bought it off the dealership floor? Whatever happened to don't buy retail?"

"You remembered," he said, smiling. "Well, I still hold to the maxim. I didn't buy it at retail. I bought it from my own dealership."

"You own a car dealership?"

"Two of them: one in Cedar, the other in St. George. Both Plymouth-Chryslers. They're doing well, too. Some of those Japanese cars coming into the market have pilfered a few sales, but I don't think they'll last. They don't make them like we do here in America."

"Now what do I do with the Fairlane?"

"I'll take it off your hands. Maybe we'll keep it in the barn. Who knows, might be a collector's piece someday." He turned to Dylan. "Speaking of the barn, I got one more present to give."

The three of us walked out to the stable. My father walked up to one of the stalls. A quarter horse mare put her head over the gate and nuzzled him.

"Oh, I love you too, Summer," he said, kissing her on the head and rubbing her neck. He turned around. "Dylan, come here for a second."

Dylan walked up behind my father. He'd never been near a real horse and was a little scared.

"No need to worry," my father said to Dylan. "This here is Summer. She's a mama horse, and just six months ago she gave birth to a baby colt. Can you see him back there?"

There was a beautiful bay roan colt with a black mane and a star on its nose. "What do you think of him?"

"He's cool," Dylan said.

"Well, I'm glad you think that, because he's yours."

"That's my horse?"

"He sure is."

Dylan turned to me. "Can I have him?"

"That's between you and Grandpa," I said. "He gave him to you."

"Yes!" Dylan said. He turned back to my father. "What's his name?"

"Well. He doesn't have one. He was waiting for you to name him."

"Can I call him Mr. William?" Dylan asked.

I swallowed. "You can call him anything you like."

My father winked at me. "You might want to think about it for a while," he said to Dylan. "A name is something you want to give a lot of thought to. Let's just call him 'Horse' for now."

"Okay," Dylan said.

Thank you, I mouthed to my father.

"Well, let's get back inside before someone catches pneumonia. I've got breakfast to make." He said to Dylan, "Would you mind going with your mom to the hen house and grabbing us a few eggs? A half dozen ought to do. There's a basket for the eggs right next to the door you walk in."

Dylan nodded. "Will you help me, Mama?"

"Of course."

It was my father's Christmas Day tradition to make us whatever we wanted for breakfast. He looked like he had bought out the local grocery store just to make sure he had everything we might ask for. He made waffles for Dylan, of course, with strawberries and whipped cream, two kinds of sausages, bacon, biscuits, ham-and-pepper omelets, and gravy. It was kind of obscene how much food he made. It was obscene how much I ate.

After breakfast my father started doing the dishes.

I walked up to his side. "I can do that, Dad. You've worked all morning."

"No. You play with your son."

"Trust me, he's played enough with me. I think he needs some Grandpa time."

As I was doing the dishes the doorbell rang. "Miche, would you mind getting that?" my father shouted from the living room. "Dylan has me all tied up here. Literally."

"Sure, Dad," I said, wiping my hands with a dishcloth. "I can't believe how many friends you have."

"You know how it is. They're like crows. I try to scare them away, but they keep coming back."

"It's probably another one of your lady friends."

I walked to the front door and opened it.

William stood in the doorway. I looked at him for a moment, then said, "What took you so long?"

CHAPTER

thirty-three

Fate's pen has rewritten more than one ending.
                                    —Elle Sheen's Diary

After kissing me soundly, William stood back and laughed.

"You were really expecting me to come back?"

"No, I didn't expect," I said, borrowing my father's words. "I hoped."

He looked in my eyes. "What gave you hope?"

"Two reasons. First, you talked with my father. My father's a smart man. He would have figured out pretty quickly that there was something between us." I smiled. "And if there's one thing about my father, the man's a fixer. He can fix anything. Tractors, dishwashers, windmills. Even relationships."

"I'll give him that," he said. "What's the second?"

"You love me."

❄

New Year's Eve was the sixth anniversary of Isaac's death. The day was even more powerful to William. It was the

270

day he had watched his friend die. It was the same day he'd been taken captive. Today it represented the opposite. It represented a new life and freedom.

It was shortly after midnight. My father had put Dylan to bed and then said good night and went to bed himself, leaving William and me alone on the couch. The room was lit by a single light in the kitchen.

I snuggled into his arms. "Do you believe in the spiritual law of restitution?" I asked.

He kissed me on the temple, then asked, "What's that?"

"It's the belief that everything we lose in this life will be returned to us in the next."

He pondered my question and then said, "I don't know." He pulled me in tighter. "But I know one thing about loss."

"What's that?"

"Whether we lose something or not, it's better to have had it."

EPILOGUE

Some own up to their past. Some are owned by their past.
The wise take what they can from the past and then leave
it behind.

—Elle Sheen's Diary

On William's and my first date I told him that I'd like to write a book someday. Here it is. At least here's part one. My life isn't over.

In spite of my rent being paid for the year, less than a month later Dylan and I moved back home to Cedar City. Saying goodbye to Loretta, Fran, Jamie, and the rest of the regulars at the diner was excruciating, with an ocean of tears, even though I reminded them that I was just moving down the road. It was a long road, but the same one passed through both towns.

Loretta shut down the diner and threw a big going-away shindig for us. My dad and William were there. Against William's advice, I tried to hook Loretta up with my father. I figured it would be like having two people I love in the same house. It didn't take. William was right. She would have driven my father crazy. And vice versa.

William and I were married in April, the same month